Englishwoman

in

Scotland

By Jenny O'Brien

Praise for Jenny O'Brien

"I absolutely adored this story. It was fun, flirty, romantic, tragic, emotionally heart-breaking at times but also very heart-warming." Kraftireader book blog.

"This author has a true gift. All her books are easy reading with a story to tell that keeps you wondering what next." Booklover Bev

"Another wonderful, romantic cosy read beautifully written with warmth love and tenderness." Michele Turner.

"She captures the reader from the first paragraph, engrossing them with her heroine's journey of love and loss, to the very end." Susan Godenzi, writer.

"Really romantic and quite sexy. Went straight on to her next book which I am just starting - an Englishwoman in Manhattan." Dawn McCaulay

Dedicated to Michelle Driscoll.

'And round his heart one strangling golden hair.'

Dante Gabriel Rossetti, 'Lilith', (1868)

Chapter One

'I'm going to kill myself!'

'Well do it quietly, darling. You know how much your father hates being disturbed before his second cup of coffee.'

'Mother...'

'There's no point in pleading. You've made your bed and now you must lie in it. Your father is adamant this time.'

The Countess of Nettlebridge beckoned to the butler with a carefully manicured hand. 'More toast please, Hodd, and you might as well bring more coffee; I fear it's going to be a long morning,' her eyes now trained on the other end of the table where her husband was barely visible behind The Telegraph.

'Yes, Madam.'

'Now, Titania, the announcement of your engagement to Viscount Brayely will be in The Times tomorrow, and I think a June wedding. That will give us three months to sort out your trousseau. Harrods, of course, and then there's the wedding dress. How do you feel about Alexander McQueen?'

'Mother, for the last time, I am not going to marry some jumped up squirt of a viscount, especially one I've never met.'

'Why of course you have. You used to play together as children.' She sighed, picking up her lace edged handkerchief and patting it to her forehead. 'It has always been his mother's greatest wish. She was my bridesmaid you know?'

'Yes, I do know. You've told me often enough,' she mumbled, staring across at her father who'd ditched The Telegraph in favour of The Guardian.

She'd always known about the close relationship between Lady Brayely and her mother but that didn't mean she had any intention of marrying her son, this boffin or whatever he was. All Google had was a brief entry on Edinburgh University's webpage about his doctorate in physics, or was it chemistry? Whilst far from stupid and a real asset at that quiz her mother had organised for homeless racehorses, she'd been far too busy at school with baking to worry about GCSE's or A Levels. With a path set out for her from childhood, one sweetened by the security net of millionaire parents, she'd done as little as possible. Watching Countdown was about as far as she went with regards to intellectual pursuits and yet here they were setting her up for life with her worst nightmare. Her and this *Lord Brayely* might speak the same language but she wouldn't understand a word.

Leaning forward she placed a gentle hand on her mother's arm. 'Please, I promise I'll be good from now on. You can rely on me. You can't just sell me off the way granny sent the family silver to Sotheby's. You just can't.'

'Now you're being ridiculous,' she replied, forcing a laugh. 'Family silver indeed. It was the ugliest epergne imaginable and don't change the subject, Tansy. The only motive we have is a wish to see you settled with some nice young man.'

'Some nice young man who just so happens to be loaded and titled. Just tell me this,' she added, lowering her voice. 'What's the going rate for an only daughter these days? Is it all about the money, or is the title everything? At the very least I'd have thought I'd be good enough to snag a prince or is it true that these days they really do prefer brunettes? Perhaps if I dye my hair black or even a striking red I might catch the eye of a count or even an earl. Yeah, I can live with that. Us blondes never seem to be anything other than blonde and it's about time I had a cut,' she said, smoothing her hand down the length of her hair. 'I've always fancied one of those pixie cuts, perhaps now is the time for a Titania make-over?'

'Now don't go and do anything stupid. Everyone, as you very well know, loves your hair. It's your trademark.'

'Well, perhaps, it's time for a rebranding. I wonder if I could sneak in a last minute appointment with Sebastian before this viscount arrives.'

She frowned, her thoughts now on why he'd agreed to such a crazy scheme.

'You haven't told me exactly why this lord wants to marry me? Why does he want to get married at all, and to someone he's never met?' She caught her mother's eye before adding, 'in like twenty years.' She tried to remember back to the visits she'd used to take with her mother but all she could remember was it was all very green and marshy. She remembered the marsh simply because she'd fallen in and nearly suffocated, or should that be drowned? Could you drown in mud? Not that the drowning part upset her half as much as the stink and the slime and then there were the frogs. She'd always had a soft spot for frogs ever since but that was no reason to go and marry one.

'Not wants to, Titania. Is going to.'

'So? Is he poor or something? Is Daddy setting a huge dowry with at least ten thoroughbreds in addition to five thousand sheep…?'

'Don't be facetious, darling. The Brayelys are loaded. They have a huge pile up in Scotland although his mother, now she's a widow, tends to spend her time between Berkley Square and the Riviera. It's so much easier to get decent staff in France,' she added quietly.

'Mother, you're not doing so badly. Hodd is a darling while Clemmy and Jessica are real treasures.'

'Treasure is the word. Do you know what the going rate for a butler is these days, darling?'

'You're avoiding my question.' She sighed in exasperation at the thought of ever getting a straight answer out of her mother. Whilst she loved her dearly there was nothing and nobody more infuriating than her mother when she set her mind on something. Usually she'd just let it be; anything for a quiet life. If she did what her mother said, what time left was her own to do with as she wished. The fact she spent it messing in the kitchen was her business. Most mornings would find her wrapped in a large snowy white apron mixing, kneading and experimenting with a variety of results; some successful, some inedible. She had a tentative plan to write a recipe book on baking, but not just any old baking book with flans, quiches and cakes; a speciality bread book comparing and contrasting a variety of sourdough and traditional yeast breads from around the globe. The last time her mother had deigned to wander down to the kitchen on some pretext or other she'd been dismayed at the sight of the top shelf of the larder cupboard and all the containers filled to the brim with all the different starter kits but, apart from slamming the door shut on her way out, she'd said little.

'What question, darling?' her mother asked, finally lifting her head from the Daily Mail, and the article on a six week bikini body. 'Do you think fifty is too old for a bikini?' she added, running a bejewelled hand over her rounded stomach.

'If I can be filmed topless there's hope for you yet, Mother.'

'Now you're being flippant, Tansy.' Her eyes still glued to the photo of Helen Mirren resplendent in red. 'You don't realise what hurt you've caused.'

'Really?' Her face pale. 'And what about the hurt to me. Have you even considered what it's like being followed 24/7 by camera toting *paparazzi* shouting 'get your titties out, Titania'?'

'Darling!'

'No.' She curled her hands around the arm of her chair as anger simmered just behind her eyes. She never lost her temper, perhaps it was time she started. Maybe it was time she did a lot more than lose her temper. Maybe it was time she put herself first for once.

'Mother, do you know why this man wants to marry me? Do you know why anyone would want to marry someone with the whole of the British media on her tail; someone whose photograph has been stamped across every rag mag from Lands' End to John O Groats? You say he's rich and titled so it's not the money or the prestige. Is he ugly, is that it? It must be something?'

She watched her mother squirm when squirming wasn't really her thing, her eyes still carefully perusing Helen's many assets. 'He's not interested in women.'

'He's not interested in women,' her voice silk soft. 'What do you mean he's not interested in women? You mean he's…'

'Oh, he's not gay or anything. It's just, he's not interested in anything unless it's in a petri dish.'

'In a petri dish?' she repeated, shaking her head. 'I don't understand. So he's not ugly. He's weird. To be honest I'd have been happy with ugly. What man spends their life with a… What's a petri dish again?'

'Oh you know, one of those agar plate thingy's. If you'd concentrated more in school and got yourself into university like your brothers, we wouldn't be having this conversation.'

'Here we go again. Tell it to someone who's actually interested. So you're happy to sell me off to the only bidder, someone who's not interested in women…'

'I didn't say that.'

'Yes you did. In fact those were your exact words.'

'Well, just think of it like this. As soon as you're pregnant with an heir he'll go back to his dishes and leave you alone.'

'Ah. The crux of the matter. So I'm to be mated like some cow in a field? I believe the term is artificially inseminated although there'll be nothing artificial about it. I'll have to put up with him slobbering all over me, buck naked until the job's done.' But her question would forever remain unanswered as her father's voice hollered from the other end of the table.

'Titania, are you still here? I thought I told you to stop badgering your mother and go to your room?' her father boomed.

'But father…'

'No buts, my gal. No daughter of mine can expect to appear on the front page of the press with everything hanging out and expect to get away with it. You're just lucky the viscount is a man of letters and therefore probably unaware of your recent debacle.' He lowered the paper with a sharp rustle. 'As far as he is concerned, you are still some sweet little thing in plaits and not some champagne swilling harpy with a large chest.'

'But they spiked my drinks, I know they did. One minute I was the designated driver and the next I knew I'd been bungled into the back of a taxi minus my blouse and shoes.'

'A likely story.'

'But a true one all the same,' her voice now only a whisper.

'Titania, you have embarrassed your poor mother and I for the last time.' He paused, running his eyes up and down her slim form. 'Your explanations don't matter. Your opinions don't matter. You don't matter. You're actually getting long in the tooth for all this gallivanting. You should thank your dear mother for arranging it. Twenty-six is shelf material you know.'

'Now hold on a minute,' her eyes flashing. 'What about Hamilton and Isaac? They're both older than me and I don't hear you nagging them to get married? In fact, I don't hear you nagging them at all.'

'Leave your brothers out of this. Men are different as you very well know.'

'Oh yeah, here we go. Men get to do what they like, when they like with whomever they like, while women are meant to suck it up with some pretentious git and get locked away to have babies. Bloody great!'

'Mind your language in front of your mother. There's no way out of this, Titania. I'm warning you. If you're not here to meet Lord Brayely for lunch, and in something other than denim, there will be hell to pay.' He shot a quick look across the table at his wife. 'You'll find we've temporarily cancelled all your credit cards just in case you're thinking of doing something stupid.'

'You've what! How dare you. That's my money...'

'No, that's your allowance I give you to amuse yourself with until you get married. You're getting married and therefore you'll be the viscount's responsibility. Any money you need ask your mother,' he added, picking up The Times and turning to the back page.

Titania looked at both her parents with a little shake of her head, struggling to understand how her life, whilst not exactly spectacular, had suddenly dissolved into a disaster zone. All she wanted, all she'd ever wanted, was a quiet life away from the limelight her parents were determined to thrust her into at every opportunity. If she had her way, she'd open up a little café in the middle of some small country village and bake cakes all day. She'd have a counter on one side for breads and one of those fancy coffee machines that pumped out designer coffee at the push of a button. But the one and only time she'd tried to discuss it with them they'd laughed in her face at the thought of her, Lady Titania, the daughter of an earl, consorting with riff raff. So, instead, she spent her days consorting with a different type of riff raff; the type that had somehow engineered the elusive and quite frankly shy heiress to disgrace herself once and for all.

She made her way into the hall, smiling briefly at Hodd as he sorted out the post onto a silver platter, a frown on his forehead. But she didn't see the frown. She didn't see anything as she tried to figure out, for what seemed like the millionth time, what had happened on that fateful night.

It had started out like any other, which made the end all the more upsetting. She'd arranged to meet a couple of old school friends for a quiet drink but, before she knew it, she'd woken up in the back of a black cab with cameras flashing through the windows as if she was somebody she wasn't. The press, all of them had her believe she'd been on a massive bender after a row with her boyfriend, some politician's son she'd never even heard of. If it hadn't been for the fatherly taxi driver slinging his jacket in front of her she'd never have been able to live it down. That crack of her father's about her chest was only partly true. There'd been skin, lots of skin but by luck more than anything she hadn't revealed much more than if she'd been lying on the beach. But that didn't matter to her father. Nothing mattered to her father more than the so called reputation of the Nettlebridges.

Chapter Two

'Nanny Mac, I don't know what to do.'

On leaving the dining room with its heavy, dark, wood panelling, she'd raced up stairs and headed for the rooms her parents had made into a comfortable bedsit for her old nanny on her retirement. Not that she'd retired, nothing like it. Far from outliving her usefulness when Titania had upped and gone to boarding school, she'd found she was busier than ever. She was the only one the master would trust to starch his collars and looking after Lady Nettlebridge's vintage collection of priceless Dior chiffon evening gowns was more than a full time job.

Pushing open the door was like a breath of fresh air as here everything was bright and light. It was all very well living in a stately home with priceless lumps of Hepplewhite, Sheraton and Chippendale but give her a large squashy sofa from Habitat any day.

Heaving a sigh, she launched herself on the couch, careful not to dislodge Haggis, nanny's old tabby, from his position in front of the fire.

She and Haggis had history, long history. He'd appeared at the door as a straggly kitten and been absorbed into the household despite her mother's preference for pedigree Persians over scrawny strays. It hadn't taken him more than a couple of swipes to put the other felines on their guard and he'd been master of the house in all but name ever since. Even the earl was known to save a couple of pieces of turbot from his plate. There was nothing Haggis liked more than a nice bit of turbot.

Tansy rubbed his ears gently before scooting to the other side of the sofa. Haggis had a long memory and he'd never quite forgiven her for dressing him up in one of her dolls dresses and pushing him around the herb garden in her pram.

'Ach, now what's troubling you,' Nanny Mac's soft lilt filling the air despite having left Falkirk over fifty years ago.

'Everything. My life is in ruins.'

'In ruins, is it? Well, you'd best tell ole nanny all about it. A problem shared…'

'A problem shared is a problem doubled,' she interrupted, unable to gulp back her tears. 'I'll just have to marry him and that will be the end of my life. There's no way he'll allow me to mess around in the kitchen, as father calls it. My life, I repeat, is over.'

'I cannae believe that.' She put down her knitting, careful to bundle up the ball of grey wool inside the half-finished sleeve. Haggis, for all his years, was still a kitten at heart and, even now, he was watching every move through heavy lids. 'So, what have they been up to now and who exactly do they want you to marry?'

'Some son of her friend; Lady Brayely. Viscount something or other.'

She scrubbed her face with her hands before accepting a tissue with the glimmer of a smile. 'I don't even know his name. So, I'm engaged to someone I don't know, not even his name.'

'Hector? Hector Brayely, well there's a thing now.'

'Hector?'

'Aye, Hector Brayely. You remember, lass, you must remember. He's the one that dragged you out of that swamp with more slime than I thought humanly possible. Brave little chap with the most amazing head of black hair. Much too serious for his own good though. Always with his head in some fancy book or other.'

'I remember, or at least I remember the slime but not how I got out. I was only little,' she added, reaching across to pat Haggis and getting a slap for her troubles. 'I must have been only four or five.'

'Four and the chubbiest little four year old imaginable. Your mother was livid, I can tell you. You were wearing a new dress bought specially. White it was with the cutest ruffles along the hem.' She paused, looking across. 'If you ask me, you could do with a few more pounds. You don't look like you know how to boil an egg let alone produce those wonderful cakes and breads you come up with. So, what's this daft plan of your parents again?' she continued, plucking at the fabric of her plain green skirt.

'They've cooked up some plan or other to marry me off and all because of that story in the papers.'

'Well, it was quite a story.' Nanny Mac tutted. 'The youth of today. Now if you'd been wearing a nice warm vest or some undergarments of any kind it would have been different. Talking of which…'

'What? Undergarments?'

'No, not undergarments, Hector. There's something…'

Tansy watched as Nanny Mac struggled from her chair, her heart dipping at the sight of her increasing frailty. Her round rosy cheeks with the blush of health were long gone, leaving in their place pale, drawn skin with a network of fine wrinkles. But the wrinkles didn't matter. All that mattered were her twinkling blue eyes with a hint of laughter in their depths. All that mattered were her soft words that could manage a whole nursery of unruly children with never having to raise her voice even one decibel.

'Here, let me help you,' Tansy said, jumping to her feet.

'That pile of magazines by the jigsaw. See if you can do a couple of pieces, all that sky is beyond me.'

'You know jigsaws aren't my thing.' She headed for the table under the window, glancing out at the carefully manicured parkland in the engaging style of Capability Brown before searching through a bundle of magazines.

'Near the top. It has a photo on the front of that girl you know; Lady Sarah something or other - the one that married the Frenchman last year?'

Tansy's eyes fell on the magazine almost immediately, drawn to the happiness that seemed to bring the faces on the cover alive. She'd heard about the wedding from a friend of a friend but hadn't really thought more of it and now here they were, and obviously besotted with each other if the smiles were anything to go by.

She shifted her gaze. She was sick to death of hearing about everyone else's happiness when her life was just about over. Her parents had well and truly scuppered any chance of escape by stopping her credit cards. She didn't have enough money left from her allowance to run away. The only hope left was that he'd hate her on sight.

'Is this the one?'

'Yes,' now just turn to the situations vacant somewhere near the back. I'm pretty certain I spotted something about a cook being needed in Oban?'

'Where's Oban and what's that to do with anything? I can't afford to get a job even if they were to pay me. I've about ten quid left to my name, ten quid to last me until the end of the month.'

'Tansy, you need to have faith. Oban is in Scotland, the place you fell in that swamp. I remember it like it was yesterday and, if I'm not very much mistaken, there aren't many houses up there large enough to employ a live-in cook.'

'So?' she said, turning the pages quickly before getting to the right section. 'What am I looking for again?' her eyes scanning down through a list of gardeners and handymen.

'Cook in Oban; live-in.'

'And why am I looking?' Her hand pausing under the only entry that fit the bill as she read out loud.

Cook required for a period of one month trial. Good remuneration for the right candidate. Live-in. Must be able to drive.

'That's the one. Now you'd best just hope its Lady Brayely.'

Tansy flopped back on the sofa, tucking her bare feet under her. 'I know I'm not the brightest in the class by a long chalk but what exactly has the advert to do with me?'

'Everything. I remember Hector as a nice boy and I'm pretty sure he'll have turned into a nice well brought up young man. Ideal husband material, and his father was incredibly good looking you know.'

'Nanny, you're as bad as my parents.'

'I'm nothing like your parents,' she tutted. 'I want you to be happy and can you truly say you're happy at the moment? Well, can you? From where I'm sitting, all I can see is a beautiful young woman still searching for that inner happiness and peace that only comes with contentment. You may hate each other on sight, but at least you'll know he's not the one. There is a chance, albeit a sliver that this will be your love match and, in the meantime, you'll be away from the watchful eyes of your parents doing what you want to, which is cooking. But, be warned. As soon as you meet him, you need to decide. You can't go on pretending to be something you're not,' she added, turning back to the front cover with a sigh. 'She looks happy doesn't she with this marquis of hers? That's what I want for you.'

'You've forgotten one thing. Whilst this Hector may not recognise me, there isn't a hope in hell Lady Brayely won't. If she's anything like mother, Hello and OK are her bedtime reading and what about references, hmm? Who the hell is going to give me a job without a reference?'

'All surmountable, my girl. You've just come out of an abusive relationship where your, er, fiancé didn't allow you to work but you have reports from the Swiss finishing school your estranged father sent you to before he died.'

'Are you sure you're not in the wrong profession? You'd have made a grand writer,' she laughed. 'And what about how I look?'

'Well, it's easy to change the way you look: a bit of dye and what about a pair of glasses? A nice pair of glasses with thick frames and even your own mother wouldn't recognise you.'

'But I have 20/20 vision…'

Even with 20/20 vision she didn't recognise the reflection peering back at her in the cracked mirror of the 08.53 from Berwick to Oban. Gone was the long white blonde ribbon of hair, in its place a long plait in a fine shade of charcoal black. She'd been all for cutting it only to back out at the last minute. She was known for her hair flowing over her shoulders in soft waves, only tying it up when she was baking and certainly never in a plait. Reaching up a hand she relished in the soft baby fine texture even as she smiled at the horn rimmed frames, circa 1960.

She'd phoned the number in The Lady under Nanny Mac's approving stare and had been amazed at the gullibility of the housekeeper. She'd lapped up her story and even promised to have a train ticket waiting at the station if she'd start out immediately. With scarcely a taxi fare to her name, she'd agreed. She'd agree to anything if it meant not being there to meet Hector like a prize cow.

Instead of spending the rest of the morning looking for that perfect outfit in which to make that important first impression, she'd nipped to Harrods and made a sizeable hole in her mother's store card. She'd had to avoid the Fashion Lab on the fourth floor simply because they wouldn't stock anything she could wear in Scotland, or at least anything an impoverished cook might wear. Nanny had told her a plain knee length black skirt was a must, probably more Primark or Marks and Spencer's than Reiss but, as Harrods was the only store card she had, it would have to do. She threw in a few plain white blouses she wouldn't be seen dead in and some thick jumpers and trousers in addition to a pair of flat black slip-ons before making her way to the 5th floor.

She'd dithered long and hard about her change in look but Nanny was right. The only way she'd get away with it was by having a complete makeover and that included hair, clothes, everything. She bundled her hair, plait and all, under the knitted hat she'd bought specially for her recent ski trip to Klosters and changed her accent from cut glass to cockney. She did get a few strong glances but they soon lost interest as soon as she opened her mouth. After that the lies came thick and fast. She was an actress don't you know. An actress with an audition for EastEnders and she had to look the part. She even managed to get the opticians to sell her a pair of frames with clear lenses from their old stock. Okay, so they were fake tortoiseshell but they certainly detracted from the cornflower blue of her eyes and the sweet shape of her face. She could almost believe she was a cook.

Making her way along the swaying carriage back to her seat she could almost believe it because it was the first time ever no one had stopped and stared. No one had asked for a selfie. No one had swivelled their head for that second and often third look. It was the first time she was invisible to anyone except herself, and it felt good. It was good. Plonking herself back in her seat she opened her bag and started rooting around for her notebook.

'I love your bag.'

Tansy's hand paused, her fingers curling briefly around her pen.

'Cor blimey, it's only a cheapy luv,' she said, throwing a smile at the woman opposite. 'Twenty-five knicker down the market,' she added, rubbing her fingers along the Chloe handbag she'd only bought last month and couldn't bear to leave behind.

'It's so realistic.' The woman sighed as she placed a banana in the outstretched hand of the toddler sitting beside her.

'I know, probably off the back of some lorry or other,' she replied, pulling out a mint instead. She might be able to pass off the bag but the Debretts notebook and gold-tipped Montblanc pen?

She couldn't believe she'd almost blown it and all over a stupid bag. There were trip wires all over the place ready for her to stumble over. It wasn't just the bag, it was everything. The way she looked and spoke were the easy part. When she'd shut the door on the sanctuary of her bedroom, she'd emptied her carrier bags on the bed and proceeded to cut out all the labels just like nanny had told her. It was unlikely someone would go looking but if they did she could always explain they were from some factory outlet or other. But she hadn't given a thought to all the other stuff. She went to pull out her Lulu Guinness make-up bag stuffed to the brim with Chanel, Estee Lauder and Mary Kay, her hand instead grasping at her phone in desperation. Okay so it was housed in a limited edition Stella McCartney case but there was nothing she could do about that as she switched it on and scrolled down the increasingly irate messages from her mother.

She'd posted her a letter from outside the train station explaining she was going away to stay with a friend for a while. When she had some money, she'd go shopping in the local market in Oban, if there was such a thing, and pick up some genuine fakes.

It was already dark, dark and cold, when the train finally pulled into the station with a squeal of breaks. The woman opposite had gotten off at Glasgow and she'd been left to her own devices for what seemed like hours. The sandwich she'd bought earlier had long gone as had the chocolate bar and mints. Now all she longed for was a cup of coffee and bed but there was still the trek up to Castle Brayely, which presumably would be in the middle of nowhere.

Jumping off the train, she threw a friendly smile at the man behind who'd foolishly offered to help with her suitcase while she struggled with her rucksack and bag.

'What you got in here, luv; the kitchen sink?'

'No. Just a few of my cookery books.'

'A cook are you? My wife is a fair good cook herself.' He smiled, his eyes twinkling back. 'Have you got someone to meet you, I'd be happy to give you a lift?'

'I'm good thanks. They said they'd arrange a taxi?'

'Ah that would be Angus. He'll be waiting outside, so. Good to meet you, lass.'

She didn't know what to expect because, despite racking her brains, all she could remember was lots of waterlogged green and marshland. The winding road leading up from the main town was a surprise but the impressive fairy-tale castle rising out of the darkness left her speechless.

Her gaze rolled over the sheer grey brick and a sigh left her lips as her imagination took over. There'd be a grand staircase sweeping down to the Great Hall. She'd be decked out in blue; a long blue chiffon gown with a wasp waist, her cleavage just peeking out the top. Her hair, suddenly blonde again, would be swept back off her face to trail down her back in a riot of curls. Her hand, gently resting on the mahogany banister would pause as her eyes snagged on the man waiting impatiently at the bottom, a man with hair as dark as…

'It's impressive, isn't it? Built in the sixteenth century by the first Lord Brayely, it stands guard over the entrance of the bay like some stern parent. It's a right shame you're seeing it in the dark though. The view over the bay is as far as the eye can see.'

'What's the other building,' she asked, her head turned to the unusual structure just visible through the cloud of rain.

'That's McCaig's Tower, well worth a visit but only in daylight. You can never be too careful, a pretty lass like you,' he said, pulling up outside and unloading her bags from the back. He shook his head when she tried to offer him some money. 'You put that away. Mr Todd will see me right.'

'Mr Todd?'

'Aye, Mr Todd. The butler.'

He frowned as she made to walk up the stone steps. 'You'd better follow me, lass. The servant's entrance is round the back. You'll be giving Mr Todd a fit if he finds you using the front door. New to service are you?'

'That's right.'

'Well, take it from me - if Mr Todd says jump, you don't ask how high. You don't need to know how high. You just jump and carry on jumping until he tells you to stop. His word is law up here but he's fair with it, mind. Just do as he tells you and you'll be fine.'

She'd be fine, would she? Her heart constricted in her throat as the reality of what she was about to do finally struck home. This wasn't a game anymore and, if she was found out, there'd be hell to pay and it wouldn't come from just her parents. She squared her shoulders and took the case off him with a sweet smile.

'Thank you for everything. I'll take it from here.'

Chapter Three

The rain of yesterday had disappeared, leaving a bright sunny morning with only a slight mist lingering over the far off islands of Kerrera, Lismore and Mull. Not that Tansy saw any of it. She'd been called at 6am with a mug of weak tea and she hadn't stopped since.

Last night was but a distant memory of half-finished sketches of life below stairs but she didn't have time to do more than save them up for later. After a briefer than brief tour of the kitchen along with the pantry and larder, there was bread to make from her favourite sourdough starter she'd been painstakingly fed ever since the Michelin chef, Louis de Gerai, had shared his special mix with her in Paris, all those years ago. She was then thrown in the deep end with preparing breakfast for all the live-in staff. After serving up six steaming bowls of porridge, she set about cooking a mountain of bacon and scrambled eggs, all served with fresh bread still warm from the oven.

With the pans put to soak in the large ceramic butler sink, she set about laying a tray for Lady Brayely who, apart from Sunday's always had breakfast in bed. There was no porridge on the dainty tray with the pristine white linen cloth and single stemmed pink rose. There was only freshly squeezed orange juice and toast with butter curls and homemade marmalade, thankfully readily available on the middle shelf of the larder along with pots of blackcurrant jam and lemon curd.

It was nearly mid-morning by the time she managed to sit down with a pot of tea and toast, not that she got much time to drink it. As soon as she'd raised the mug to her lips she'd been summoned upstairs to the second sitting room to meet her ladyship.

With a quick look in the small mirror by the baize door that separated the servant's quarters from the rest of the house, she followed Mr Todd's straight back into the hall.

The Dowager Viscountess, Lady Brayely, whilst not a carbon copy of her mother was of the same type, a type Tansy had been manipulating for years. But, in this pale yellow, south-facing room, she suddenly realised she had no power here. All the power was sitting behind the bow-fronted Regency desk with not a hair out of place on her carefully blow-dried bouffant-topped head. Here, she was less than the pale yellow rug by her feet and certainly a lot less than the two terriers stretched out in front of the fireplace.

Dropping a small curtesy, she waited, but not for long.

'Ah yes, Miss, er, Smith. It is Miss, I take it?'

'Yes, Your Ladyship. Tansy Smith.' Now she wished she'd come up with something a little more believable than Smith but it would have to do.

'Well, Miss Smith, welcome to Brayely Castle. Todd has, I'm sure, shown you the ropes?'

'Yes Mam.'

'Work hard and, if the bread this morning is any indication of your cooking skills, I'm sure we'll be delighted. I'm out this evening but I'd like a nice piece of fish for lunch. I'm also holding a dinner party this Saturday for twelve, if you could have a sample menu worked out by tomorrow.'

'Yes, Mam.'

'That will be all.'

Lady Brayely waved her hand dismissively, the height of rudeness but Tansy headed for the door all the same, her mind awash with meal ideas.

After lunch she was taken on a tour of the house and gardens by the housekeeper, Miss

Campbell. She wasn't allowed in any of the main bedrooms on the first floor, only shown where they were in case she ever had to deliver trays. The second floor was taken up with bare rooms put aside for the nursery and playroom. There was also a billiard room and mini cinema as Lady Brayely couldn't abide noise. The servants' quarters were on the next floor and then the attics, which remained locked, as did the doors to the six turrets.

'We don't go up there much, only to sweep occasionally and check for birds although the view is amazing from the top, or so I'm told.'

Tansy looked enquiringly at the quiet woman by her side, clad in plain grey with a bunch of keys hanging from a lanyard around her neck.

'I'm scared of heights.' She headed back down the stairs, her flat pumps gliding across the polished wooden floor with scarcely a sound. 'I'll show you the herb garden and the vegetable garden, that is if Jock isn't around.'

'Who's Jock?'

'Jock is the head gardener and the bane of my life. He may have worked here since he was a boy but it's as if he owns every carrot and sprout. You just be giving your vegetable order to Mr Todd and he'll see you get what you want. There's chickens too so there's always fresh eggs. The butcher delivers three times a week but if there's anything special you'd like, although I do pride myself on keeping a well-stocked larder.'

'I can see that, Miss Campbell. I was thinking of using those sausages tonight as her ladyship is out. What about a nice *toad in the hole* with some *lemon meringue* for afters?'

'That will do just fine. I'm not sure when his Lordship will be back but Master Tor likes a nice well-cooked sausage.'

'Master Tor?'

'Yes. You know. His lordship - I can't seem to get my tongue around it yet,' she said, pushing the heavy wooden side door open before leading the way over the gravelled path to the back, and the gardens beyond. 'I've known the master since he was in breeches running amok, scaring the chickens.'

Tansy blinked at this new bit of information although it didn't do much to clear matters in her head. She'd been reluctant to ask about Hector, seeing as he was probably still up in London for their date. She wondered what he'd thought when she hadn't turned up, just as she wondered what excuse her parents had come up with. But these thoughts were only fleeting; she'd been far too busy getting her head round this new life to think about him more than that.

'You mean Lord Brayely?'

'Aye that I do. The new Lord Brayely. Lord Hector Brayely but he's been called Tor since he was a wee bairn. His father, God rest his soul, was lost to us a little over a year ago. Drowned on the Loch he was; a great tragedy.'

It was all very nineteenth century with 'master this' and 'lady that' but who was she to question any of it? She couldn't begin to guess at the staffing costs what with the butler and housekeeper, not to mention the live-in ladies maid. They didn't have a housekeeper at Nettlebridge Manor but then again the manor only had eight bedrooms. The castle must have twice that number and all ready in case guests decided to stop over at the last minute. Apart from Nanny and Hodd, and the woman that came in from the nearby village of Amberley, they managed between them. Her mother was a great one for outside caterers and, on the rare occasion they had more than a couple of guests, that's what she did.

Wandering around the neat rows of early potatoes, she introduced herself to the head gardener. She could see for herself she wouldn't be allowed loose amongst his carefully weeded borders. Standing by the side, a pipe in one hand and a spade in the other, he looked more like a beggar in his grubby denims and patched jacket but there was a twinkle lurking somewhere under those bushy eyebrows as he followed Miss Campbell's retreating back with his eyes.

Stepping across, careful to avoid stepping anywhere near anything that might be a plant she held out a hand and introduced herself with a smile.

'English are yeah?'

'That's right. Just outside London. I don't know much about living in the country or growing vegetables so I'm relying on you to help me with what's in season, Mr Jock. There's a dinner party on Saturday, what do you recommend?'

That evening she served up steaming plates of toad in the hole with fresh coleslaw and rocket salad and was pleased to note the quiet smiles of satisfaction on the faces of the three remaining members of staff sitting around the table, especially when they spotted the lemon meringue pie and jug of fresh cream for afters.

Sitting down opposite Mary Doyle, Mrs Brayely's maid/secretary, and between Mr Todd and Miss Campbell, she let the conversation flow around her. There was talk about the dinner party in two days' time and who'd been invited.

'I posted out the invites earlier,' said Mary, in between mouthfuls.

'Go on, do tell? The McKay's, I'll bet. She was around at theirs last month and she'll want to show off her new cook,' said Miss Campbell.

'Yes, the McKay's and that daughter of theirs. She's back from that cruise.'

'God, she's awful. If there was ever a woman with her hooks into the master its Cassandra McKay.'

'Now, now, that's just gossip,' interrupted Mr Todd. 'It's nothing to do with us who his lordship goes out with.'

'Hmm. You won't be saying that when she makes him sell up and spend the year on the Riviera; snooty piece and a trouble maker to boot. Who else Mary?'

'Well, there's the Houston's just back from their trip to The Med and then the Marshalls. She always invites them, and then the vicar and his wife. But she's only included them to make up numbers,' she added for Tansy's benefit. 'She's asked for the rubies from the bank and I'm to press her black.'

'That's enough!' came the now not-so-quiet voice of Mr Todd. 'Thank you, Miss Smith for such a delightful supper. You'll have to excuse Mary, she's still very young. Here at Castle Brayely we do not gossip.'

'Yes, Mr Todd,' trying not the laugh at the feel of Mary's foot kicking her ankle. 'Anyone for some shortbread?'

She spent the remainder of the evening sitting at the scrubbed pine kitchen table thumbing through the selection of dog-eared cookery books she'd brought with her. She hadn't been lying when she'd told the taxi driver about the contents of her suitcase. Apart from jeans and the clothes she'd bought in Harrods there'd been little room except for her books and as for her rucksack… Instead of the usual truckload of make-up and jewellery befitting a lady, she'd used the majority of the room for a Tupperware box full of yeast.

She'd decided on a Scottish themed menu using the home grown produce available. There was one thing she wouldn't compromise on and that was the inclusion of the seasonal vegetables Jock had shown her earlier. The red cabbage looked delicious while the Jerusalem artichokes were just about ready. The fact she'd never had to cook one was another matter but one she wouldn't let bother her more than that.

The clock was chiming midnight when she finally set aside her pen and stretched. It was all very well feeling useful for a change but it came at a cost. She still hadn't recovered from the train journey and, with a full day of work under her belt, all she was fit for was bed.

Heading for the Aga she placed a small copper pan on top, half-filled with milk. A mug of cocoa sitting in the comfy chair by the stove would be just the thing to help her drift off to sleep.

The sound of a door banging followed by a muffled curse jerked her out of her sleepy state. Taking a shaky breath she tried to think up one thought that didn't shriek out burglar. She was all alone on the ground floor with no one either awake or within shouting distance. Her eyes shifted to the poker conveniently placed next to the grate and, before she even knew how brave she was, she'd grabbed it with both hands and was creeping towards the scullery and the noise.

Her first thought was he must be a very inept burglar. Either that or he wasn't really a proper burglar; just some chancer seeing what he could pilfer on his way home from the pub. Well, whatever or whoever he was, he was in for a shock.

She was a stealth warrior, she told herself. She was a stealth warrior sneaking up on her prey, and she would use everything in her power to stop him laying his thieving mitts on any of Lady Brayely's silver. She struggled to suppress the sudden hysterical laughter building in the back of her throat as she remembered the feelings of inadequacy and desperation she'd felt in Rome last year when someone had managed to con their way into her hotel suite. Luckily she'd been out and, apart from her clothes, there hadn't been anything of great value to steal being as she wasn't one for diamonds and pearls. But just knowing someone had rifled through her things was bad enough. Just knowing someone had invaded her personal space had her racing back home with, if not her tail between her legs, then her feathers decidedly ruffled. That's why she couldn't believe what had happened to her in London. She couldn't believe one of her friends would have spiked her drink, but it was too much of a coincidence for *all* the *paparazzi* to converge outside The Golden Potato nightclub in Chelsea. Were they even friends? She'd known them for fifteen years but did she really know them?

Standing there with the poker raised she didn't see the dark shadow; the extremely large and threatening dark shadow. She didn't see anything except her own demons from the past.

Chapter Four

'Who the hell are you?'

Growing up in Brayely Castle as an only child amongst all the grown-ups, he'd spent most of his time fishing in the loch with his imaginary friends.

He had many imaginary friends mainly because they protected him from the ghosts that roamed the castle, especially at night. Not that he believed in ghosts more than that. The creaking and groaning just under his window came from the shutters mounted high on old rusty fixings which, if not as old as the castle, were certainly long overdue an upgrade. The cold wind screaming through the corridor when he pattered back from the antiquated bathroom in his Noddy slippers was just that; wind. It wasn't some spectral being out to scare him witless but that didn't stop him from peering over his shoulder as his walk turned into a run.

When he was a little older, he'd searched his father's library for everything and anything he could find on the topic of ghosts. From what he could gather, as he sat curled up in one of the sofa's, his Star Wars clad feet dangling over the arm, was that ghosts didn't exist, or if they did no one had actually proven it. As an impressionable ten year old, he didn't want to think about the subject more than that. It wasn't that he'd ever actually seen one. He'd no more seen a ghost than he'd caught that twenty foot pike in the lake his father kept moaning about every time he returned with an empty bucket. If he'd tried to catch it once, he'd tried a thousand times until that last time…

He didn't like to think about that last time and the lonely rowing boat abandoned in the middle of the Loch. They'd found him eventually washed up on the side of the bank. A heart attack, a massive heart attack that he wouldn't have known anything about until it was too late, was the only good thing to be had from the episode. It would have had to have been massive to topple his bear-like father, a man he'd thought invincible. He'd grown up then. A little late for a thirty-three year old, but a grieving mother in addition to the sudden responsibility of the estate certainly aged a man well beyond his years.

He was now a year older and ten years more serious but that didn't mean he believed in ghosts. The wind still whistled up the corridor and the shutters still rattled but, just as he'd discarded novelty footwear in favour of dull brown moccasins, he'd also discarded his night-time fears. In truth, he probably owed his love of discovery to his former ghost hunting self. All those hours hidden away in the library, he'd quickly moved from the paranormal to the normal, devouring quicker than chocolate buttons the rows upon rows of heavy tomes his grandfather and then his father had owned. He believed in the benefit of research. He believed in unravelling the truth and finding new truths from an assimilation of often previously unconnected facts but that didn't mean he believed, or would ever believe, in ghosts.

So, if he didn't believe in ghosts, he'd very much like to know who the pale woman standing in front of him brandishing what looked very much like one of the crested cast-iron pokers dotted around the place was. A thief? A visitor? Or, his eyes wandering over her denim clad person and scruffy trainers, a member of staff? God forbid!

He'd have to speak to his mother about employing anaemic and, it must be said, unstable maids if the glint in her eye was anything to go by. She looked in need of a square meal or two in addition to a week lying somewhere hot with a Campari and soda in her hand, his attention again drawn to the poker and the pointy end still pointing in his direction. Of course, he wasn't scared of her or of what she was clutching in her tight fists being as he was probably twice her size. He wasn't scared of her but the sight of her worried him all the same. There was something about her, something just outside his range of vision like one of those words just on the tip of his tongue even as he felt something heave in his chest. Either he was about to have a heart attack or he was attracted to her, more than attracted as he spent precious seconds examining his feelings before slamming the door shut on any emotion apart from curiosity.

Glancing up at her face he wondered for the first time if she might be scared? After all, he was far from catwalk material dressed as he was in head to foot black leather and, to her, he was a stranger. He wanted to let her off the hook, he really did. However he was quite keen to see what this ghost of a girl was made of; this ghost of a girl with eyes trailing memories of clear summer skies in their wake.

'I asked you what you were doing here.'

'No, you asked me who the hell I was. Right back at you mister.'

'Actually it's not mister,' his voice soft. 'It's professor.'

'Really? Professor of what exactly?' One hand now on her hip, the other still in possession of that ruddy poker.

'Mycology.'

'My what?' She frowned, her nose wrinkled up in thought. He liked her nose.

'Is that something to do with bacteria?'

'No, that would be bacteriology, or the broader heading of microbiology, if you'd prefer?'

'I'd prefer if you'd shut up with all the facts and, instead, tell me what the hell you're doing in my kitchen well past midnight?'

'Your kitchen is it, lass?' he replied, slipping into the textured brogue of his forefathers. 'Wait until I tell her ladyship the hired help are getting ideas above their station,' his eyes insolent in their renewed study of her face and then her body before finally meeting her gaze. 'You do know Lady Brayely, my mother, don't you?'

He'd have felt sorry for her then if he wasn't trying to work out how someone so pale to start with could lose all colour completely. If he wasn't tired from his journey after that aborted attempt to meet the woman his dear mother had set her heart on as a daughter-in-law, he'd have let her down gently. If she thought it her kitchen, presumably she was the new cook in a long line of cooks and it never did to upset the cook; one never knew what they might do to the food before it arrived on your plate.

'How do I know you are who you say you are?' she countered; her frown back.

'Oh, I really wouldn't go there, er, Miss-?'

'Smith.'

His eyebrows shot up. 'Well, Miss Smith, if you could drop the poker I'd be most obliged. I'm tired, hungry and in no mood for mind games with the staff. Go to bed. Mr Todd will answer all your questions in the morning,' he ended, heading for the larder with a dismissive flick of his hand.

No one knew more than him the difficulties his mother had in getting any kind of help this far north but *Smith*? He'd have to have a word with her in the morning and remind her the last time she'd employed someone off the street, they'd been found at the bottom of the hill with a sack full of her collection of priceless Crown Derby Imari porcelain. He'd bet his Mitsubishi she didn't have a reference to her name or a clue how to run a kitchen…

He eyed the fresh loaf of bread with surprise as he tried to remember how long it had been since there'd been anything other than supermarket sliced white at the castle? Probably six months, ever since Mrs Brodie had decided to hang up her apron and retire to Inverness. He'd make himself a cheese sandwich with a large whisky on the side while he tried to forget the creamy texture of her skin against those celestial blue, almost grey, eyes. He could forget himself in those eyes although, by the pull of her mouth and the sound of the poker being hurled back into the coal bucket he was easily reminded he was off women, now more than ever if the last twenty four hours were anything to go by.

He should have stood up to his mother. He should have said what he'd wanted to. There was no room for a woman in his life. Work was his mistress just as work was his bedfellow. They were more trouble than they were worth with their tantrums and demands. Apart from that one early hiccup, he'd managed to avoid the lure of a fine pair of eyes or the pull of softly rounded curves, his mind scuttling back to the sight of her slim form with bumps where bumps were meant to be. He shook his head. The one thing he'd been unable to avoid was the tearstained pleas from his recently bereaved mother.

She loved him and, now there was only the two of them, he'd been spending more and more of his time up here managing the estate as an excuse to keep an eye on her. The excuse he'd given for resigning from his full-time teaching post at Edinburgh University was only partly true. Yes, he'd be able to finally finish his book on the role of mould in the origins of the species just as he'd have much more time to pursue his own research into one particular mould. But he'd managed to do both, up to a fashion, during the long holidays. The truth was, he was increasingly worried about leaving her alone. That and the renewed interest of his female students into the state of his personal life now he was a lord left him handing in his notice with little or no regret. He still gave the odd lecture and still retained use of his flat on campus but he was now his own master.

'There's a nice piece of Mull cheddar or Lanark Blue if you'd prefer? Did you want your bread toasted or?'

'What?' He receded backwards, bending his head to avoid banging his head on the door frame. 'How did you know I was looking for…?'

'Cheese? I have two brothers. They're always looking for cheese, although there's some toad in the hole left if you'd prefer?' she added, pulling the door of the Aga open. 'I was going to take it down to Jock in the morning but I can always rustle up some more. Apparently he likes toad in the hole.'

'I'll bet he does.' His eyes wide at the sight of the still puffed up batter glistening with fat sausages. 'That looks wonderful. Join me in a whisky?' he added, pulling a bottle and a couple of glasses off the shelf and placing them on the table. 'I really do hate eating alone,' which was a lie if ever there was one. He had no thoughts on whether he had company or not but mostly he was quite happy eating with a book propped open on the table in front of him. He'd only said it as a sort of apology because, funnily enough, he felt he owed her one. She'd probably, for all her bravado with the poker, been scared witless at being disturbed so late. And then his train of thought led him to think: what did a cook need to do at midnight? The kitchen looked pretty much as usual with its heavy pine cupboards and plate racks full of freshly washed dishes so if it wasn't cooking… His eyes landed on the papers lined up beside his glass, papers that worryingly looked like dinner party menus.

'Just a small one then, it's not my favourite.'

'You haven't tried a glass of Oban single malt then, I'm guessing?'

She'd placed a steaming plate in front of him with a couple of ramekin dishes on the side, one with tomato ketchup and the other mustard. There was also a plate of freshly cut bread that would do any doorstop proud. He smiled at the ketchup before dipping the end of his fork in. 'You're the first cook I know that will allow this stuff on the table willingly.'

'My brothers eat it with everything, sir.'

He frowned 'I see they've trained you well, er, Miss Smith.' He caught her eye. 'Is there another part to your name or should I insist that you call me Lord Brayely? My name is Tor.'

'It's Tansy, Tansy Smith.'

'That's unusual. Tanacetum vulgare from the aster family if my memory serves me correct. Good as an insect repellent but toxic in large quantities,' he added with a quirk of his eyebrow. 'Are you toxic in large quantities, Tansy?' His eyes flickering back to the poker. 'Good meal though, I certainly can't fault your cooking, and as for the bread… What yeast did you use?'

'What yeast did I use?' her reply faint.

'Yes, yeast woman. I'm a mycologist, remember? As a cook you'll know that yeast is a fungus? The difference is easy to see in the cellular formation, with yeasts not having the filament strands found in the more popular types like mushrooms for example,' he said, waving his fork in the air before diving in to spear the final sausage. 'Of course, yeasts and fungi are only a fleeting passion. I'm a mould man really.'

Chapter Five

'I'll give him toxic in large doses,' she muttered under her breath.

'What was that, lass?'

'Nothing Mr Todd. Just talking to myself.'

'Nothing wrong with that, nothing at all. Breakfast in half an hour?' he added, taking the keys to the cellar from the hook behind the door.

She'd walked into the sparkling kitchen a couple of hours ago, expecting to find a pile of dirty dishes waiting for her, the same pile she'd seen scattered across the table when she'd finally left him to the rest of his whisky. He'd washed up and even put away his dishes in addition to hanging the tea towel by the Aga to dry.

Slamming the dough out on the freshly floured board she started kneading and pummelling the mixture, all the time imagining it was his neck under her hands as she squeezed and then stretched the sticky mass before finally shaping it into recognisable loaves.

She placed the trays by the Aga and remembered that neck and the tight cords of muscle disappearing under the collar of his jumper when he'd finally thrown away his jacket. He was built like a well-fed tree trunk and, if he hadn't turned out to be an arrogant son of a bitch, she'd have found herself drawn to him.

Up until now she'd favoured slight, effeminate types with a wardrobe from Tom Ford and hand-crafted shoes from Italy. But there was something about the way his thick wavy hair, as dark as a raven's wing, complemented his piercing blue eyes, eyes that seemed to follow her every move with a supercilious glint. His skin was dark too, almost swarthy and a little weather-beaten, if truth be known. Here was a man who didn't bother what he looked like if the state of his holed Guernsey was anything to go by. Here was a man who wouldn't dream of putting anything on his face other than shaving foam and perhaps the odd dab of aftershave as she recalled the slight scent of musk with a slight tint of man when she'd placed the plate in front of him.

Time was shifting under her feet and she only had ten minutes to finish the porridge before the staff descended for their breakfast.

Lifting the heavy skillet, blackened with both age and use, she added oil before layering slices of thick bacon against the glistening surface. She was pleased she'd come, more than pleased as she reminded herself to text Nanny just to let her know all was well. It was the best thing she could have done.

If she'd met him across the table at the luncheon party her parents had arranged, she'd have been fooled by his looks. He had manners, good manners in addition to looks to burn and she'd have been fooled into falling for him. She'd have probably married him too, if his behaviour had continued. She'd have married the most conceited, egotistical, selfish tosspot she'd ever had the misfortune to come across. The only good thing about him was his looks and his skill with a dish mop – not enough by a long way as she gave the porridge a final stir.

She'd thrown together potato cakes earlier and now, with the bacon well under way all that was left were the eggs; the eggs she'd gathered first thing when the dawn wasn't even a distant golden glimmer on the horizon. Her mother would have disowned her if she'd seen her bundled up in an old mac and even older wellies she'd found by the back door. But here in the Highlands, fashion didn't matter as much as comfort or at least it didn't when she was seeing to the chickens. She'd thought she'd see quite a bit of polite society coming and going during her stay but, now she knew she wasn't going to touch Lord Brayely with anything approaching a wedding band on her finger or a veil on her head, she wasn't sure just how much she'd get to experience. There was Saturday's dinner party to organise but after that she'd probably make up some excuse and race back to London.

Staring up at the clear dark sky, she suddenly felt sad at the thought of leaving. There was something here in this lush green landscape with the only sound coming from the crunch of frost underfoot that was penetrating through the wall of the well-bred young lady she'd surrounded herself with like a shield. Here, society didn't matter. Here, what she looked like, as long as she got the job done, didn't matter. Nothing mattered apart from the small role she had to play in the continued running of the castle on the well-oiled wheels Lady Brayely demanded. The ideal would be if Lord Brayely disappeared in a puff of smoke, back to wherever it was he'd come from, leaving her to carry on just as she was doing until she got fed up with the solitude and loneliness.

Up until now she'd always been surrounded by friends. People she'd allowed into her inner circle. People she'd trusted to keep her confidence while they happily allowed her to pay for everything. But after recent events perhaps they weren't really friends? Perhaps they just viewed her as a cashpoint? There was no perhaps about it.

Heading across the lawn to the chicken coop situated through the arch at the back of the vegetable patch, her mind was full to the brim of flickering pictures from her recent past. All the time she'd wasted on impromptu shopping trips. The summer trips to the Caribbean followed by the must have winter ski trips, always staying at the most expensive resorts. In truth, all she wanted, all she'd ever wanted, was to be left alone to her own devices but they hadn't let her. They'd wanted to party with a capital P and, as she was the only one with enough money, they'd told her exactly what she'd wanted to hear.

Just one more drinky. One more pair of Manolo Blahnik's and you can never have too many Hermès handbags, dahling!

But here, opening the wooden door just as Jock had shown her, all that mattered was the sight of twelve eggs nestling in the straw. If farming and the like was this easy she might even take it up seriously, although she couldn't imagine her parents eating any eggs other than those that came pre-packed with the Waitrose logo on the top.

'His Lordship. He's back. Came in late last night by the sound of that bike of his purring up the drive. You'd better cook some extra bacon. Our Master Tor likes a nice bit of well-done bacon,' Mr Todd said, walking into the kitchen and heading for the sink in the corner to wash his hands before joining the rest of the staff.

She smiled to herself while she added this snippet of information to the virtual catalogue she was creating in her head.

Tall, dark and handsome professor; into mould, whisky and bacon seeks like-minded woman for fungal frenzy.

She'd pass this time, thanks all the same.

'I'll get right to it, Mr Todd. He might like some mushrooms too?' she added, thinking of the basket she'd seen in the larder earlier, as she carried the heavy pot across the room.

'I'm sure he would. Her ladyship has also approved your menu,' he said from his position at the head of the table.

She felt everyone's eyes land on her as he continued speaking. 'I can't help telling you I was a bit afraid, you being a Sassenach and all. If there'd been any salmon or clootie dumplings you'd have been on the next train out.'

Tansy nearly dropped the bowl she was holding. As it was, it nearly toppled out of her palm. Correcting it with a nervous hand she finally managed to lift off the lid and start ladling porridge.

'Is that right?' Her eyes firmly fixed on the pot. 'I'd never have chosen salmon and clootie dumplings. I'm not sure I even know what a clootie dumpling is,' she added, lying through her teeth as she continued passing out bowls into waiting hands. She hadn't known what they were until last night when she'd added them as the ideal dessert for a Scottish dinner party. It was still only March, after all and the hearty fruit-laden dumplings had sounded just the thing to see the guests on their way. But that's all she knew. The lord of the castle obviously knew better.

She got that he was trying to help, she really did. He must have spotted the menu on the table after she'd left him to his whisky, and had decided to put his own stamp on her carefully thought out celebration of all things Scottish. What he'd done by the sounds of it was tear her carefully penned efforts to shreds and start again with some concoction all of his own. The only problem was how the hell was she meant to know what to cook if she didn't have a copy? Telepathy?

'Her ladyship likes good plain cooking,' he continued. 'That rhubarb crumble was a stroke of genius. It's the master's favourite; always has been, ever since he was a wee bairn.'

'Oh, I love rhubarb crumble,' Mary interrupted. 'Reminds me of me ma's cooking back in Dublin. Go on, what else will there be?'

'Well let's see,' she said, resting her chin in her hands. 'I'd really like Mr Todd's opinion on where best to buy the er…'

'Trout or the scallops, lass?'

'Both, Mr Todd. Both. There's nothing like a nice bit of trout with scallop.'

She knew she'd got it wrong by the look on his face but it was too late to do anything other than brave it out.

'Ach, you haven't been forgetting so soon? Your scallops on brioche sound wonderful, but her ladyship prefers her trout just baked with almonds, plain and simple. Don't be going changing a thing now will you?' His eyes on her face before throwing a look across at Miss Campbell.

'Er, no, Mr Todd. Scallops with brioche, fresh trout with almonds and rhubarb crumble, got it. I'll make some shortbread and perhaps a few chocolates to go with the coffee?'

He nodded his approval, pushing his bowl out the way before reaching for the toast while she dished out the potato cakes with fried eggs on top and a sliver of bacon, before starting on Lady Brayely's breakfast tray.

'What time will his lordship want his breakfast?'

'Good morning, Toddy.'

'Good morning, sir. It's a fine day after all that rain,' he replied, laying both The Times and The Telegraph beside his side plate. 'There's porridge and tatty scones this morning,' he added, placing the toast rack on the table alongside the silver teapot.

Tor lifted up the pot and poured himself a cup before replying. He should have left the whisky alone after that first glass but he'd forgotten both the time and the possible hangover as he puzzled over what must be the worst Scottish menu he'd ever seen. She wasn't Scottish so it wasn't her fault, he'd said to himself as he'd flung the ripped card into the Aga and closed the door. She wouldn't know about farmed salmon and the benefit of a nice piece of freshly caught trout with the taste of the wild still lingering in its plump flesh. And as for Clootie pudding; he'd never met anyone that actually enjoyed eating it. It was reminiscent of all those Christmases long past where he'd been told to eat what was in front of him or go hungry and, being as stubborn then as he was now, he'd chosen the latter. His parents weren't to know he'd learnt very quickly to keep both the cook and the butler on his side so that there was always a slab of chocolate cake waiting for him in the pantry. As he'd grown older, the cake had changed to thick sandwiches and a pot of coffee on the Aga for those evenings he'd crawled home in the middle of the night, or should that be stumbled?

'I haven't had a tatty scone since June retired,' he said, scraping the bottom of his bowl clean before making room for the plate Mr Todd had ready for him. His eyes widened at the sight of the large lightly browned potato cake mounted with a perfectly fried egg with the yolk just the way he liked it. There was even a pile of crispy bacon layered like a train track and pots filled with mushrooms, maple syrup and ketchup.

'You just wait until you've tasted this. June was a fine cook but this is something else.'

'Well, it certainly looks good enough to eat,' he said, picking up his fork with gusto. 'So how's she getting on then, this, er, Miss Smith is it?'

'She certainly knows a thing or two about cooking that's for sure. She's game too; I'll have to give her that. She was up at the crack of dawn gathering the eggs when I'll bet she doesn't know one end of a chicken from the other.'

He joined him in a laugh as he sliced his bacon before assembling the perfect mouthful of bacon and scone, dipping it in his egg yolk and finally adding just a drizzle of syrup.

'The hens are still laying then?'

'Aye, twelve perfectly formed ones this morning. She's using the rest in a cake for afternoon tea.' he added. 'You're mother's invited Colonel Romforth.'

'Oh God, has she? Thanks for the heads up, man. I'll happily leave them to their own devices, so. Tell her I'm fishing, will you, if she asks.'

'Trout?'

'Trout, although I'm not promising. They haven't been biting much lately.'

He placed his knife and fork in the centre of his plate, his gaze shifting from the tall dignified man dressed in sombre grey and out through the tall leaded windows recessed into the brickwork. He loved the view from the front of the castle, the outstanding Sound of Kerrera drawing his eye across to Mull and the Morvern Hills beyond. But he loved the view from the back the best. The rolling lawns pulling away from the shingled paths for as far as the eye could see. The neat flower beds bare but for the odd early daffodil and snowdrop brave enough to poke their heads through the still hard ground. He could even see the loch in the distance through the trees against the backdrop of Ben Cruachan's shrouded peak towering over the neighbouring hills. It was here, with nature all around, he'd first discovered his interest in fungi.

It had all started with one mushroom bloom he'd found nestling beside the net of his football goal, a mushroom he was determined to eat for his supper until his father took him aside and explained about the dangers of eating just any old random fungi. They'd sat together in the library pouring over the many photographs his father had found in one of the books that used to belong to his own father, a keen botanist. It was here he'd learnt how to recognise a mushroom he could eat and one that could kill.

His world from that day became narrower, his vision tunnelled inwards to life and the world that happened underfoot. He started to crawl around on his hands and knees in the shrubbery, much to the annoyance of his mother and all the trousers he holed at the knees. But he didn't care. His football was long forgotten. His football posts relegated to one of Jock's shed's until they were finally donated to the local school.

All he was interested in was right here in his back garden and, apart from the odd fishing trip with his father or trouser buying trips to town with his mother, his life was a journey of discovery. A degree in microbiology was a given, a doctorate in mycology with a dissertation in mould and its uses in medicine, a must have. An honorary fellowship at Edinburgh University was an honour but anything that took him away from his microscope for even one second was a hardship he was determined to avoid. There was life outside his obsession. He went on the odd drinking forage into Oban and Edinburgh but, now in his thirties with his mates all partnered off, the calls to beer were few and far between. There were women; like-minded scientists where long discussions late into the night sometimes ended in a bedroom romp but oftentimes didn't.

His mother was worried about him: she wanted grandchildren but not only that, she thought him lonely.

Was he lonely, his eyes landing on a sliver of orange just peering its nose out from the long undergrowth? Were there times when he'd like the feel of another presence in his bed, someone to chat to as well as to cuddle? If that was loneliness then, yes, he was lonely. His gaze stilled, his attention now focussed on a flap of wing just visible through the arch leading to Jock's vegetable patch and all thought left him, apart from just one.

'Did you say she collected the eggs this morning?'

'Aye?' his voice questioning.

'That's what I thought.' He stood up, tossing his linen napkin on the table before hurtling towards the door. 'I'll bloody kill her. Toddy, get the shotgun. The chickens are out and there's a fox...'

Chapter Six

'But I didn't know...'

'But you should have known. Which planet was it exactly you were born on, Miss Smith? Obviously one that doesn't have foxes perchance? We lost the whole stock last fall, probably to the same blighter, which is why we have a top of the range chicken coop with reinforced wire fences set into concrete footings. Our chickens are the safest in the whole of Scotland, that is until some stupid English twit comes along and forgets to close the bloody door.'

He was absolutely livid. She could see it in the way he wouldn't even meet her gaze and the way his hands were fisted on probably the largest shotgun she'd ever seen, but that didn't give him the excuse to be rude.

'That's racist...'

'What? You're English, aren't you? What's racist about calling a spade a spade? You can call me a Scot if you like, I certainly won't take offence,' he said, with a slight softening in his manner, so slight you'd barely notice. 'In fact I'd take it as a compliment.'

They were standing head to head in the middle of Jock's vegetable patch with everyone available from Mary, the two cleaning women from the village and Mr Todd in addition to Jock trying and failing to round up hens that didn't want rounding. The fox, thankfully, had disappeared into the undergrowth after a couple of shots over his head but he was probably only waiting until their backs were turned before continuing on his rampage.

'It's the law of nature anyway,' she added, heading to the left to try and herd off the largest bird, obviously the ring leader.

'What's the law of nature exactly?' he snarled, joining her in trying to manoeuvre her into a corner between the shed and the manure pile.

'Well, he must be hungry.'

'Hungry? Are you mad, woman or simply deranged? It wouldn't be quite so bad if he just killed the one but he doesn't. He never does. A fox will kill the lot if he gets the chance, sometimes up to thirty in a single frenzied attack. He'll just leave the bodies and walk away for us to find later. Law of nature, my foot.'

'I didn't know.' She waved her arms, directing the now flapping chicken towards him. 'So why didn't you just shoot him then?'

'Because, Miss Smith that would make me as bad as him. It's March, breeding season. He probably has a pile of cubs hidden away somewhere and, despite what you might think of me, I'm not a murderer,' he ended, missing his footing and landing on his back with a large thump and an even larger expletive.

They both turned to watch the chicken strut away in the opposite direction with a flick of its tail feathers.

'This is useless, we're getting nowhere.' He scrambled to his feet with a frown as they both watched Jock and Mr Todd herd the smallest, a pretty bantam with pale golden feathers in completely the wrong direction.

'What do they eat?' she asked, holding up her hands to ward off any roars coming in her direction. 'Apart from scraps that is. If we could just lure them back...'

'Lure away, Miss Smith. There's a bag of chicken pellets in that bin over there.' He pointed to the black dustbin beside the shed with the pointy end of his gun. 'I'm going to enjoy watching this.'

'You could help?' she mumbled, grabbing a handful before heading towards a large fat orange bird and throwing a pellet in her direction.

'Come on boy, time for lunch.'

'Er, since when did you ever know a boy to lay an egg, Miss Smith?'

'Shut up, and why you can't call me Tansy like everyone else, I don't know,' she hissed.

She made the fatal mistake of taking her eye off the chicken while she turned to look at him. He was laughing now, his head rolled back, exposing a column of thick neck. And suddenly she wondered if the rest of him was as brown or was it just because he spent so much time outdoors? Her eyes, glued to his throat, didn't spot the chicken peer across at the pellet before taking a cautious step.

Tansy was more interested in the breadth of his shoulders under the thin sweater he must have worn down to breakfast and what might be underneath than in some irritating, badly behaved hen. She was more interested in the lock of hair that had curled up across his forehead and suddenly a picture of a little boy, a lonely little boy running wild in the grounds with grubby cheeks and even grubbier shorts invaded her thoughts to the exclusion of all else.

She knew she was staring but that didn't matter. Whilst she was still fascinated by, what was after all, a hunk of a man, her mercurial thoughts now pulled her in a completely different direction. Maybe there was a reason for his arrogance? Maybe his childhood, in this amazing part of the world, had been a lonely isolated one? There would certainly have been few children to play with, if any, apart from at school and she could imagine someone with such an unusual interest in fungi wasn't going to be that popular. His mother hadn't struck her as the most demonstrative either and a child needed that. They needed a lot more than bricks, mortar and open spaces.

Her own childhood hadn't been perfect by a long way. As the youngest with two older brothers, she'd been treated as a baby long after she'd outgrown both pull-ups and pigtails. But, despite the age gap, she'd remained close to both her brothers and they were always there if she needed them, particularly Hamilton. She'd always been closer to Hamilton than anyone until he'd left for university and then left for good. If he'd been less tied up with work she'd have sought his advice over her recent setback but he wasn't so she hadn't. Perhaps she should have and then maybe she'd feel less confused about the man in front of her; the man now staring with that horrid sneer obliterating any trace of recent laughter. Maybe just maybe she'd misjudged him? Maybe just maybe she'd misjudged herself?

Her mouth dry, she decided to ignore him just as she was going to ignore the blush racing up her neck. She continued muttering soothing encouragements to the chicken, the very female chicken but her heart wasn't in it. This was her fault. She only had herself to blame. If she hadn't left the stupid door unlatched she'd have been in the nice warm kitchen making lunch.

'I don't believe it, it's actually working,' his whisper causing her to tilt her head in the direction of the steady stream of birds following the trail like well-behaved school children on their way to assembly.

'Of course it's working, I never doubted it for a second,' she said firmly, heading backwards in the direction of the coop where Jock, ever quick off the mark, had the door open and a handful of pellets as a reward for each bird as she hopped through the opening.

They all sank down on the lawn to catch their breath. Two hours of chicken hunting had proved just how unfit they were and just how smart the chickens were.

'Look at the state of me.' Tansy tried to brush the soil and dirt off her jeans but only succeeded in spreading it. 'If I'd known, I'd have worn my Fitbit and racked up a few thousand steps. Her ladyship will want her lunch and I've nothing ready.'

She wiped her hand across her face to ward off the tears brimming on her lashes but only succeeded in knocking off her glasses. But she didn't care. She'd only been here two days and she'd made a complete hash of everything. There was no lunch prepared. She had guests for afternoon tea and a cake half mixed on the table not to mention bread in the Aga that would now be burnt to a crisp. She hadn't even thought about supper and then there was the dinner party with no menu to speak of. She might as well just leave on the next train because, despite failing at her one attempt at independence, she'd done what she'd set out to and that was decide Lord Tor Brayely was the last man on the planet she'd marry, not that he'd asked her. He'd no more want to spend another five minutes in her company than he would marry her; not now.

'Ach, don't be worrying, lass. Her ladyship will understand once she hears,' Mr Todd said.

'There's no need for her to hear about this because I certainly won't be telling her. She left straight after breakfast, isn't that right, Mary?' Tor interrupted, jumping to his feet.

'That she did, sir. Off to the hairdresser and then coffee in town. She won't be back for a good half hour or so.'

'Just time for me to get cleaned up and then I'll take her to The Manor House for lunch.' He smiled, a gentle smile that lit up his whole face. 'She has a thing about their ox liver and bacon, and I'm sure the staff will be happy with a scratch lunch so that you can crack on with your baking. Oh,' he paused, his eyes careful to avoid her tear stained cheeks. 'The colonel loves cherry cake and those little cakes with icing that taste of almonds?'

'Bakewell tarts?'

'Bakewell tarts. I'm quite partial to a tart myself, a Bakewell tart,' he added with a wink. 'If you could put a couple aside?'

'Won't you be there?'

She knew she shouldn't have asked the moment the words left her mouth. As the hired help, it was none of her business whether he'd be there or not. It was her job to cater as if he would be. That was all. She felt the heat build in her cheeks but instead of dropping her gaze she lifted her chin and waited for his caustic reply. But all he did was shake his head before turning on his heel.

Back in the kitchen, she threw together a batch of French gallettes. Yes, it was the wrong country but it only took seconds to make the batter and she could easily get the staff to help her fill them with whatever toppings they wanted when they joined her for lunch. She then turned her attention back to her cake as she let her mind wander.

Her first thought was she liked him. Her second; she liked him a lot. Yes, he'd been horrible to her, more than horrible but the sad truth of it was she deserved everything he'd said and more. Those poor chickens. If it hadn't been for him spotting them, she'd have had a lot more to worry about than getting tea ready. And then to take his mother out to lunch so she wouldn't have to hear about what a mess her new cook had made of everything. She could have hugged him there and then, although she wouldn't. However, now the seed of thought had been planted, she wondered what he'd have done if she'd thrown herself into his arms and given him a proper thank you. He'd probably have just stood there, his arms by his side with that sneer on his lips she was growing to hate. Yes, better she remembered her place and started making tentative plans for her return to London. She'd proved to herself once and for all marriage to him wasn't an option, hadn't she…?

Dusting the cherries with flour so they wouldn't sink to the bottom she realised she hadn't thought of London even once. Apart from a brief call to Nanny, she hadn't spared a second for her friends and what they were up to. She hadn't even bothered to flick through Mr Todd's pile of newspapers to see whether she was in them, usually one of the first things she did each morning. London seemed so far away. It was far away, over five hundred miles away to be exact and she was quite happy about that. She could honestly say there was nothing about it she missed, not one single thing. Well, apart from her bespoke hand-stitched silk and cashmere mattress that is. If she hadn't thought it would give the game away she'd have had it shipped up for the duration of her stay.

She didn't see him for the rest of the day or the one after; the day of the dinner party but she was too busy to notice. No, that wasn't quite true, she amended, taking a sip from her mug before it went the same way as the last one; cold. She'd noticed, but she didn't want to.

He'd left a bucket full to the brim of plump, glistening trout but he didn't come into the kitchen, instead handing it to Jock to take in for him. She'd heard via Mr Todd that he'd wolfed down her steak and kidney pudding in addition to the small plate of Bakewell tarts as if food was going out of fashion but that was all.

The next morning was one of those clear fine days with a dollop of spring flickering around the edges; a life reaffirming day where hope was in every little thing from the struggling sunlight dappling its gentle glow to the stalwart daffodils nodding their regal golden crowns in the gentle breeze. Winter would soon be a long distant memory she thought, sniffing the crisp air; crisp air with a lingering sting of ice in its tail.

She'd woken up early and, wrapping herself in a thin dressing gown, raced downstairs to put the kettle on the hotplate before heading back for a quick shower. Everything was quick; it had to be if the list of tasks she had to undertake was to be completed. The first one, of course, was collecting the eggs, something she did with a sense of nervousness. She must have gone back to check the little gold plated sliding bolt five times just to make sure before picking up the wicker basket and heading back to an already stewed mug of tea.

She'd have loved to have abandoned her day, a day which would see her pinned to the kitchen like something from a nineteenth century workhouse. She'd love to rest her arms on the moss covered wall by the castle's stone pillared entrance and just bide awhile, her eyes seaward towards the islands beyond.

Islands she wanted to see before she had to leave. But she didn't. This dinner party had to be perfect down to the last glass, polished fork, immaculate table linen and floral centrepiece. It had to be perfect, not for Lady Brayely and certainly not for Tor. It had to be perfect for her, just her, because it might very well be the last dinner party she had sole control over.

Before she knew it, the clock had ticked its wearisome way full circle round to 6 pm. The bread rolls were in the oven just as the scallops were resting in a covered glass bowl on the table. The rhubarb crumble was in the larder and the trout all ready to pop in the Aga when the time was right. Cooking and baking was all about timing, something she'd learnt the hard way in France, the happiest of months up until that last day.

Monsieur De Gerai had been a hard task master but then she hadn't expected anything less. She hadn't expected to fall in love with both the city and its people either. She'd felt independent and free for the very first time, free from all the boundaries an aristocratic upbringing brought. Her parents were happy, more than happy she was both out of their way and safely under the thumb of someone they both knew and respected. She'd have stayed if her life hadn't turned out to be an illusion.

She'd have stayed forever, instead of running away. Yes, she'd learnt a lot during her stay in France, and most of it not about the art of cooking.

Time was now on fast forward and she needed five minutes, just five minutes to wash her face and change into one of the white blouses and plain skirts she'd bought in Harrods. She marshalled Mr Todd to keep an eye on everything while she went to check on the table in the dining room, ignoring his look of manly horror with a gentle laugh. She wanted to tweak the trailing flower arrangement she'd made from bits and pieces from the garden she'd gathered earlier. There'd been few flowers to speak of but she'd managed well enough with ivy, fern fronds and strands of heather. But now she wanted to check that everything was just so.

Running into the room she skittered to a halt at the sight of Tor, standing in front of the fireplace while he fiddled with his tie.

'Bloody stupid thing. Of all the contraptions known to man I just don't get the bloody bow tie. If I'd known she'd insist I wouldn't have agreed to attend.'

She must have moved because suddenly he wasn't staring into the mirror but swivelling around to face her, a rueful grin on his face.

'Sorry, I didn't know...'

'Please don't apologise. I know all about men and their relationship with the *'bloody bow tie',* she said with a smile. 'I've brothers who could never manage either. They were always nagging me to help.'

'Well, come on then.'

Her eyes widened. 'Come on where?'

'Help me sort it out.' He must have caught her frown because he was in front of her, his hand dangling the offending article from the very tip of his fingers, his gaze roaming over her face, her lips, her neck before finally meeting her eyes with a sheepish grin.

'Please, Miss Smith, would you do me the kindness of helping me with this blasted thing?'

'Certainly, sir.'

'The name is Tor.' He faced her, the tie now dangling around his neck.

'And mine is Tansy,' she replied, reaching her hands up.

'Ah yes, Tansy one of the most dangerous of...'

'I'd be very careful if I were you,' she said, pulling none too gently on both ends before starting to fold. 'It would help if you could bend your knees or something,' she added, standing on tiptoe as she tried to pull the satin fabric into shape.

'Ha, I'll just bet you'd love me to go on bended knees…' he said with a chuckle but he crouched down all the same before adding, 'This is really kind of you.'

'I'm not being kind.'

'What?'

'I said, I'm not being kind. As lord of the manor and the son of my employer I'm just doing what I'm told,' she said, finally tweaking the tie in place. 'There, you're all done,' she added, turning towards the table and moving a fork a centimetre to the left before shifting her hand towards the floral centrepiece.

She felt his presence a second before she felt his hands mould themselves over her shoulders, forcing her to turn around and face him. One hand moved, circling and then lifting her chin so that she was forced to meet his eyes. It was meet his eyes or close them and there was no way she'd close them, not now. Not with him. Not ever.

'Oh, I don't think I'm done, Tansy. In fact, I'm far from done. As the hired help is being so accommodating I can think of a raft of other things you can help me with…' he said, lowering his head a whisper away from her lips, his breath stroking her skin like a caress.

And suddenly she wanted him. She wanted him more than she'd wanted anything in her life. She wanted the weight of his lips on hers delving, devouring, consuming and not just his lips as his hand shifted from her shoulder to curl around the base of her neck. Yet how could that be? How could she want him, she puzzled, trying and failing to concentrate on her breathing as his fingers left the safe confines of her skin to pile drive through her hair? How could she hate him, all of him, and yet want him with a desperate passion that defied all sense? He was her worst nightmare, wasn't he? He was the sort of man that was prepared to get himself married to someone he'd never met all because she had the right parentage. And he wouldn't be faithful, her mother had been completely wrong on that score. He wouldn't be faithful if his current behaviour was anything to go by. At the first sight of anything in a skirt he'd be off trying to play parlour games with the maid or, God forbid, the nanny if they ever went on to have children.

Her heart skipped a beat even as her hands bunched into tight fists. No, she couldn't allow herself to like someone like him, someone that tried it on at the first opportunity. She hated him. She hated all men like him and she should know as a sudden picture of Monsieur de Gerai appeared before her eyelids. Monsieur de Gerai, the man her father had entrusted with her wellbeing. Oh, she knew all about positions of trust and the way men broke them as soon as their wives were out of the way. She hated him, even as his lips shifted that final distance and smoothed themselves over her flesh with a soft grunt.

Her eyes flickered closed despite themselves, her long lashes splaying out over pale cheeks even as her heart twisted under her ribs. His lips, gentle at first wavered as if they too were finding their way but soon the gentleness faded as the pressure increased and she was lost. His tongue, probing, insistent, firm, finally breaching all her defences and her legs would have buckled if he hadn't shifted his arm from her head to her waist. Her hands, unfurled pressing against the hard muscle of his chest, his warmth permeating through her fingertips as wave after wave of emotion assaulted her.

There was joy, helplessness, fear even before anger took over and, with anger came the strength to resist, to push away. *'How dare he'* was her final thought as she dragged herself off him with some herculean effort, well-hidden underneath her size eight build.

Bending over, her hands on her knees she stared up at him, her chest heaving underneath the confines of her t-shirt. She didn't care about anything other than the need to get away but, first, he was going to get a piece of her mind.

'If you put even one finger on me ever again I'm going to report you for molestation. What the hell gives you the right to touch me anyway?' she railed, her eyes flashing silver shards of grey behind her lenses, her hands now on her hips. 'What, you behave like this with all the cooks, is that it? Is that why your mother has difficulty in getting anyone to work for her, because of her son's wandering hands?'

He laughed. She couldn't believe that he actually threw his head back and laughed,

'I'm sorry; it's just that… if you saw the last couple of cooks, ninety if a day, you'd understand…'

'I wasn't expecting you to take it as a joke. There's nothing to laugh about here. Absolutely nothing.' Her eyes devoured him, unshed tears glistening on the end of her lashes proof of her anger if the bright red slashes across her cheeks and heaving chest weren't enough of a sign. 'Your mother is expecting dinner to be served shortly. What should I tell her when she complains it's late, that her son couldn't keep his hands to himself?'

'Hey, that's not fair…'

But she didn't listen. She couldn't listen because if she did, she might just be tempted to run back into his arms and claim what was, after all, rightly hers. Instead she hurried towards the door only to pause at the sound of his footsteps stopping inches behind her.

She focussed all her attention on the wood, the moulded panelling in shades of mahogany ingrained with the mark of time over its mottled surface. She felt his breath again on her neck and a shiver ran across her skin. A shiver of anticipation, of fear – she didn't know but he must have seen it because suddenly he was stumbling back to the other side of the room. His voice when he finally managed to speak was barely a hoarse whisper dragged up from some unknown place deep inside.

'Look, I'm sorry. I apologise, alright. I thought that you, that we…' He stuttered to a halt. 'I didn't mean to offend you.'

She finally turned, her gaze hovering over him with the best imitation of distain she could come up with as she forced her eyes to shift up and down his body with a curl of her lip that her mother would have been proud of.

She'd learnt a lot from her mother as a child, most of it of little importance and most of it stuff she would never do but the art of putting someone in their place once learnt could never be forgotten. She'd never done it before, she'd never had either the need or the nerve but, as an experiment, it worked a treat. She watched the colour flush across his cheeks as he dropped his own eyes from hers to stare at the floor.

Her work here was done. Turning on her heel she catapulted up the stairs with the devil at her back, unaware he'd moved to the doorway to watch her every step.

She'd have been worried then if she'd seen his expression change. The stain of embarrassment faded only to be replaced by puzzlement and then a smile. If she'd seen him strolling across to the drinks tray and pouring a large whisky with a cheerful whistle she wouldn't have bothered to change into her cutesy black skirt and lawn blouse. Instead she'd have flung what she could into her case and escaped into the night.

Chapter Seven

The whisky didn't help, but then dinner parties weren't really his thing. Sitting at the opposite end of the table to his mother, he wished himself elsewhere. Anywhere would do but preferably not anywhere near the new cook until he could think through that little scene in the peace and quiet of his own drawing room. Steepling his fingers, his elbows resting on the snowy white linen, he'd just had the best scallops of his life and yet all he could think about was the woman slaving over a hot stove while she delivered food with the precision of a Michelin ranked restaurant. He should really be throwing out the odd comment to the vicar's wife on his left but she was in the middle of explaining the details for the forthcoming fete, a staple summer feature not least because the funds raised were already earmarked for the new church roof.

Shifting his eyes to the right was the wrong thing to do because his mother had, in her wisdom, plonked Cassandra McKay on his other side.

It wasn't that he didn't like her. He was ambivalent if anything. Oh, she was alright to look at if voluptuous brunettes with acres of creamy white cleavage were your thing. But he'd always been of the opinion less was more in these social gatherings and, if truth be known, he didn't know where to look. He had a pretty good idea where she wanted him to look. He had a pretty good idea she'd be more than happy if he didn't just look, the way her hand seemed to touch his knee and beyond with a degree of familiarity well outside their previous history. But simply put, he wasn't interested. He'd never been interested. He would never forget the way she'd used to ignore him and, in a small community like Oban, she'd gone out of her way to have nothing to do with him. It was only since his father had died and he'd become Lord Brayely that he'd started bumping into her. Funny that!

'Would you like a top up, Cassandra?' he asked, lifting the wine bottle and shaking it.

'Only a smidgeon. We're walking down the hill later and I don't want to fall in a ditch now, do I? Although,' her lips pouting, 'I'm sure you could find an inchy winchy piece of bed for me in this little ole castle. I'm not really equipped for the walk in these heels,' she added, lifting up her red skirt to reveal six inch stilettoes.

'I think not. I'm sure Todd will be happy to give you and your parents a lift at the end of the evening.'

Cassandra laughed, a tinkling sound that went right through him. He'd been prepared to forget the cleavage more suitable for page three than a sedate provincial dinner party but that was until he'd heard the laugh. He'd forgotten until that moment just how irritating it was. He'd forgotten until that moment just how irritating she was, irritating and persistent as he felt her hand flutter to his knee again and up along his thigh.

'A lot can happen between then and now.' Her hand inching its way onwards and upwards. 'My, what big thighs you've got, Lord Brayely.'

'And not just big thighs,' he muttered, clamping his hand back over hers and removing it before tilting his head in the other direction. 'Mrs Houston, how was your trip to The Med?'

'Oh, absolutely delightful, Tor. We moored in *Villefranche-sur-Mer*, so much more refined than *St Tropez,* don't you know, and the beaches… Long sandy stretches for as far as the eye can see. Of course, we did pop into Nice and Cannes once or twice for the shops but we're getting a little past it for all that nightlife.'

'Surely not?'

He repeated the expected drivel he'd been brought up to quote at length all the while watching as Mr Todd carried in a large dish of trout and then vegetables.

As he'd expected, it was cooked to perfection; the lightly toasted almonds just glistening through on top. He was glad of the respite from having to field Cassandra's red tipped claws from his nether regions, both of her hands now busily slicing through her full plate reminiscent of a builder tucking into a fry-up. What with starting off a conversation with the Marshalls on wine it was dessert before he finally built up the courage to renew their conversation.

'I couldn't possibly eat this; rhubarb at a dinner party, so stodgy and so bad for the figure,' she added, pulling her dress down over ample hips to the detriment of any last vestiges of decency where her chest was concerned. He'd already overheard Mrs Pounder, the vicar's wife, gently remonstrating with her husband twice on where he should and shouldn't focus his gaze.

'Some cheese and biscuits then, Cassandra,' he asked, flicking a look in the ever watchful Todd's direction. 'Do try some of these oat cakes; the new cook is a marvel.'

'She certainly is. Wherever did you get her?'

'You'll have to ask my mother that, I don't involve myself with the intricacies of staff employment.'

'That's why you need a woman to guide you. You can't expect your mother to do it, not at her age.' There was that laugh again and, had she just insulted his mother by calling her old?

Looking at the clock on the mantelpiece, he couldn't believe it was only 9.30 but at least he'd be able to get rid of her for a while. Old rules died hard in these parts and it was still customary practice for the men to have their coffee and port served at the table while the women had theirs in the drawing room…

'Well, my boy, that was a delicious meal, probably one of the best I've ever tasted, although don't be telling Agnes,' the vicar said on a smile as Todd went to top up his glass of port. 'I hear you have a new cook. A good cook is worth their weight in gold, I can tell you.'

'Indeed.'

'Will she be popping up or…?'

'Oh, I don't think so. She's probably exhausted. This is her first dinner party and she's only been here a few days.' It was a long established custom at Brayely Castle to summon the cook at the end of the meal but, with the taste of her lips still fresh on his mouth, she was the very last person he wanted to see.

'Perhaps on Sunday then?' His eyebrows shot up. 'I take it she will be attending church?'

'I can't really say.' He wandered over to the fireplace on the pretext of adding a log to the glowing embers.

Would she even be here tomorrow? The way she'd reacted to what was, after all, only a kiss was a little extreme to say the least and it wasn't as if he'd lunged at her. Oh, he knew that's how she'd decided to play it; all that bluff about being assaulted by the lord of the manor. He'd never assaulted anyone in his life, certainly not a woman. That was all a smoke screen to disguise the fact she'd been an equal partner in the kiss. Okay, so he'd initiated it but she'd kissed him back with equal measure. He hadn't expected that, not from a woman like her.

He frowned. Now why had he added that rider? A woman like her? Like what? What was she like, exactly? She certainly wasn't all she seemed, that's for sure. For a start, just who in their right mind dyed blonde hair black? No woman he'd ever heard of. It was the other way around surely? But, there at the base of her neck fine pale, blonde hairs peeking out from that creamy white skin. And it wasn't just her hair. It was her accent and the way she glided around the room as if she'd been taught to walk with a book on her head. Deportment, that was it. She had deportment and an accent with a distinct variability in the use of the humble H, which she seemed to drop whenever she thought anyone was listening.

He swivelled the deep red in the bottom of his glass as he remembered what he'd forgotten and suddenly he didn't know what to think anymore. Placing his glass on the table he turned towards the door with a brief apology and headed to the hall and then outside and around to the back of the house, the view now shrouded in darkness.

He remembered the shiver and the way it had rippled across her skin, her paler than pale skin and now he questioned everything that had gone before. Every glance, every laugh, every snarky comment between them had led him to think she'd felt the same way. For all his bravado at her having kissed him back, what if he'd been wrong? What if he'd taken advantage of her, knowing all too well if she objected it would be her job? But he wasn't like that, was he? She'd fancied him. He knew it just as if she'd said the words. So why was it now he felt the biggest heel imaginable? Why was it he wanted to apologise, not once but a thousand times and yet he wouldn't. He couldn't. He couldn't bear to see that look on her face again; that stare of pure loathing, a shiver of revulsion on her skin. He'd caused that, only him.

'If you're sure you can't find room for little ole me…'

They were standing on the top step, Cassandra's hand clutching on his arm.

'Now, what would your father say, or my mother for that matter?'

She laughed. 'They'd both be delighted. Mater has been trying to marry me off for years and as for your mother: she's always going on about the importance of family,' she added, tracing a finger over his cheek. 'Just think of all those little Tor and Cassandra's running over the place.'

'Who said anything about marriage, Cassie?' he said, resorting to the childish nickname he'd used to call her in her pigtail era.

'Now that's not very nice,' her head twisting to look at something over his shoulder. 'Who's that? She looks familiar?'

Tor tilted his head and together they watched Tansy stroll across the lawn, the moon reflecting off her white blouse, turning everything to silver.

'The new cook, Miss Smith.'

'Really?' She turned back, losing interest. 'Will I be seeing you tomorrow at church?' She pouted, lifting her face with a kiss; a kiss he sidestepped so it avoided his mouth.

'Probably.' He gave her ample bottom a playful slap. 'Now, off to bed before I change my mind.'

'Promises, promises. Sleep well,'

He couldn't sleep. He tossed and tumbled around his mahogany-framed four poster bed for what seemed like hours, finally drifting off when the first shards of grey, blue sky were starting to flicker over the horizon. He awoke mid-dream with his heart hammering in his chest and the image of her expression imprinted on his vision. He was a cad, a bounder, a scoundrel. He'd thrown himself at one of the servants. She was in his employ and therefore under his protection and he'd nigh on attacked her like some toff from the last century – or should that be the century before? She must have been scared witless because, despite her show of bravado, she was a mere slip of a thing and he was twice her size. If he'd wanted to do a lot more than kiss, there was very little she could have done to stop him.

He only descended to breakfast when he knew Todd would come looking for him. Church was a mandatory requirement he had to undertake when he was in Oban whether he liked it or not and something he was only prepared to do on a full stomach.

Piling his plate with bacon and eggs he wondered how she was this morning. Had she had trouble sleeping or had she snored her head off as soon as her head hit the pillow? She'd have been tired that's for sure because it was nearly 11 o'clock by the time they'd finally exited the dining room and there'd still have been the remainder of the dishes to wash not to mention the table to set for breakfast. She'd have been up at the crack of dawn for staff breakfasts too, he thought pouring himself a cup of tea from the fresh pot Todd had just put in front of him.

'My mother is late?'

'Aye, she's decided to have breakfast in bed even though it's Sunday. She'll be in time for church though.'

'Oh. Everything alright downstairs, Toddy? The staff certainly excelled themselves. That meal was delicious.'

'Aye, everything's fine. I'll pass on your compliments to Miss Smith, shall I?'

'Yes, please do,' he said, well aware of the slight censure in his tone. He knew he'd broken with tradition by not inviting her up to thank, but to hell with him and to hell with her. It was about time they actually realised just who the boss was.

He picked up a slice of toast and added it to his side plate, his hand hovering over the little dish of butter curls while his mind hovered over his next choice of words. He was happy to break with tradition but some things were sacrosanct and church was one of them.

'Will the staff be attending church as usual? My mother and I will be happy to make do if it helps?'

'It's no bother sir. Miss Tansy will be going to the evening service. She volunteered.'

I'm sure she did, but he left the words unsaid. If she was going to avoid him that was fine by him. In fact it would make it all so much easier. *In fact*, he'd make it easier still, picking up his phone and scrolling down the list of meetings he hadn't been going to attend.

'I'll be popping up to Edinburgh for a few days so there's no need to cater for me. I'll let my mother know when I'm expected back.'

It was very easy to avoid someone when they wanted to be avoided but that didn't stop her from missing him all the same. Her eyes flew open at the thought even as she forced her attention back on the bowl and the pile of potatoes she was peeling for lunch.

He'd been gone a week, one of the longest weeks ever. At first no one had told her he'd gone, and why should they? Why indeed? After all she was a nobody; a two bit cook on the minimum wage. Oh, she was living in the lap of luxury in the most amazing castle in its own grounds. The prestige. The honour. The reality of such a privileged lifestyle accounting for quite a few thousand off the final salary or pension scheme (of which there was none).

The truth of it was, the castle, whilst amazing was situated off the beaten track and was as draughty as hell (that is if hell had drafts). The windows rattled in their frames at the slightest provocation, not to mention the wind whistling up through the floorboards. She'd taken to wearing both her woolly hat and socks to bed and if there'd been such a thing as a stray cat lurking, she'd have locked him in her bedroom to wrap around her feet. But there were no cats, only Lady Brayely's terriers, of which she saw little. If it had been up to her, she'd have one of those large dogs that were more sheep than canine. All that wool snuggled up next to her would be better than any hot water bottle. She blinked as the vision of Tor wrapped around her invaded her head, Tor with long taut legs binding her to the mattress. She wouldn't be in need of any additional heat source if she had him to curl up to, she thought, raising a hand to her suddenly flushed cheek.

How the hell could she think of him like that? The only obvious answer was one she didn't want to hear but one she couldn't close her mind to. The thought, once it gained a foothold, swept through her body like a lightning bolt before heading straight to her heart where it could wreak maximum damage. She didn't despise him. She found him fascinating, distracting, attractive even but she didn't despise him.

She despised Monsieur de Gerai with a passion and he'd had good looks to burn. She remembered his smouldering, tawny brown eyes and tumbling, brown hair he'd had cut professionally every few weeks or so. His designer clothes were carefully chosen for impact over comfort. His teeth, by God she'd hated him but she couldn't fault his whiter than white teeth, which must have cost thousands to cap and polish. It was his skin, no not his skin, she added, twisting the peeler in order to dig out a couple of eyes. It was the feel of his skin that last night when he'd found his way into her bed. The way he'd smoothed his hands over her thigh, caressing places she'd never been touched.

She'd been asleep, dreaming even; dreaming of being in bed with a man, which was strange in itself because up until then her dreams had always involved something to do with food. She was an eighteen-year-old baking-obsessed child-woman with little or no interest in anything outside of baking so her dreams weren't going to be a surprise. And then hovering on the edge of reality she'd finally realised that it wasn't a dream. It was her worst nightmare, a nightmare that wasn't going to stop anytime soon if the feel of his leg pressing between hers was anything to go by.

So no, she didn't despise Tor; she was attracted to him even though it was madness and yet... If that kiss was anything to go by, they had a lot more in common than their titles and wealth. They had chemistry, or whatever the word was for the mini explosion that had stopped her in her tracks and made her forget everything and anything except the feel of those lips weaving their magic across her heart. She just couldn't understand it. Yes, he was good looking in that rugged Heathcliff kind of way but certainly not her type.

Perhaps it was his mind she was attracted too, a dimple appearing. He was intelligent and his mother adored him, which was probably a bonus.

The truth was, apart from that one accident by the chicken coop and that one incident in the dining room, she knew little about him. And yet... She placed the final potato in the waiting colander all ready to rinse and rested her elbows on the table. And yet she knew he smelt of sandalwood mingled with a hint of outdoors. She knew his hands weren't smooth; they were rough in places. Workers hands, even. He wasn't bothered about clothes either, unless he had a wardrobe of designer clobber stashed up in Edinburgh and she just couldn't see it. She also knew he liked animals, all animals, as she remembered he'd been careful to shoot over the fox's head. But all those things didn't amount to much. She should hate him. She should hate the type of man he was; the type of man who'd allowed his mother to choose him a wife. What man in their right mind would ever do that, unless he was gay?

She laughed, lifting the colander off the table and taking it to the sink. He wasn't gay! He was a hot-blooded man who should have been able to get off his backside and find himself a mother for his future heir because that's what this was all about. She was under no illusions he actually wanted to get married. He'd make her pregnant and then leave her to rattle around in Oban while he carried on chasing fungi. It was probably a bonus he fancied her enough to actually want to sleep with her, but might that not be more down to the fact she was forbidden fruit? Would he still want to sleep with her if he actually knew who she was? Perhaps he made a habit of sleeping around with all and sundry? Perhaps a ring on his finger wouldn't secure his fidelity? What if she married him only to discover he was playing away from home? What then, and more importantly what could she do about it? She'd probably be pregnant, pregnant and dependant.

Her pace quickened but not so fast that she could outrun her thoughts. Today was her day off, or at least what was left of it after she'd made the potato salad. She'd been up at the crack of dawn but, after she'd finished the salads to go with the sliced meats she'd arranged for lunch, she was free until Mr Todd bolted the side door at 11pm. Washing her hands in the little sink by the back door she undid her apron and hung it on the hook by the larder before grabbing the coat, hat and gloves she'd brought down with her. She didn't bother looking in the mirror, there was little point and, with the red and orange stripy hat pulled well down, even her own mother wouldn't recognise her. She had her wage packet in her bag and a need to go exploring but first there was one thing she had to do.

'Mother, don't cry.'

She'd followed Craigard Road down the hill, past McCaig's Tower but she didn't loiter like she wanted to. Asking for directions at the bottom she found a public phone box sequestered away at the back of the post office. She wasn't up to date on mobile tracking but she was pretty sure she shouldn't use her own phone to call her parents.

'But darling, won't you tell us where you are? We're worried about you, and Nanny said you didn't even take your purse?'

'Well, there'd be little point with daddy stopping my allowance.'

'He didn't mean it. You know your father. His bark is always so much worse than his bite, and those photos of you semi-naked really upset him.'

'They upset him, what about me? How do you think I felt, huh?'

'Don't, darling. You have money in your account so why don't you get the next plane home and we won't say any more about it?'

'I'm not ready to come back yet; soon but not yet,' she added, tilting her head to look across the bay and towards the islands; islands she intended to explore. Perhaps not today but on her next day off she'd get up early and catch the ferry across to Mull. She bit down on her lip as she pondered whether to ask the next question, a question she desperately wanted to know the answer to and her reason for phoning.

'So what happened to Lord Brayely then, did he turn up and does he still want to marry me?'

'He turned up. Your father handled things like he does. They went away to the study and parted on the best of terms.' There was a sigh down the line. 'He wouldn't stay for lunch, said there was little point and after I'd gone to the trouble of ordering in those cheese soufflés your father likes so much.'

Tansy gripped the phone as she wondered just what her father had agreed to in her absence. She wouldn't put it past him to have accepted his proposal on her behalf. If she went back to London she'd probably be bundled off to the nearest registry office before being whisked off somewhere on baby making duties.

Taking an uneven breath, she decided to probe a little deeper. 'And what did you think of him, still happy to sell me to him like a sacrificial lamb?'

'Now, darling, be serious. You know we only have your best interests at heart.' There was a pause. 'If I'm honest, he was a little scruffy for a viscount. I was expecting a suit and I got head to toe leather. I was tempted to check his credentials. Nanny liked him though.'

'Nanny was there?'

'Oh yes, she said she wasn't going to miss it for the world. She plonked herself in the hall with that black felt hat on her head and her bag clasped to her chest on some pretext of having to post a letter when she knows Clemmy takes the post every morning on her way to the butchers.'

Tansy hid a laugh. Good old Nanny. At least she'd now be able to find out the truth.

'I see you've been up to your tricks, old girl.'

'Now, now Miss Tansy you have some respect for your elders. Old girl indeed,' but the softness in her tone belied her words.

'So what did you think, Nanny?'

'I think you need to get yourself back here and stop gadding about. Your father is storming about the place threatening to call the police. Your poor mother has wept a mountain of tears while that so call friend of yours, Miss Julietta, has been on the blower every five minutes trying to find out your whereabouts.'

'You didn't tell her anything did you?'

'What do you take me for? I never did know what you saw in her.'

'I'm beginning to wonder myself.' The image of Juliette's sniggering face was one of the only things she could remember from that night. She was the only one who knew her plans for the evening and she had every opportunity to spike her drink. Swallowing the sudden lump blocking her throat she carried on.

'So, I hear you met Lord Brayely?'

''Aye.'

'Come on, Nanny, spill the beans.'

'He'll do you fine so he will. A fine figure of a man. He'll make a good dad.'

'I don't need a dad, one's bad enough.'

'Not for you, for your children.'

She laughed. 'You seem to have made quite a few plans for me while I've been away.'

'And why wouldn't I? You haven't the sense you were born with. He'll do you fine, more than fine. He's kind and well-mannered...'

'You seem to have found out quite a bit about him. Just how long were you speaking to him?'

'Not long, but long enough. I dropped me glove and we got chatting like. A serious young man if ever there was one, but the serious ones are the best. He'll be faithful, mark my words.'

'Yeah, right,' she said, remembering the kiss. She couldn't very well forget it. She'd been dreaming about it, about him, ever since.

'You just need to get back here pronto, Miss Tansy. There's no point in staying now you've met him. What's going to happen if he finds out, have you thought about that? He'll think you've played him for a fool and, believe me, he may be many things but a fool isn't one of them.'

She finally said her goodbyes and, placing the phone back on the cradle, walked across the street towards the promenade to watch the ferries and fishing boats make their way out to sea. But she didn't see the boats with their distinctive bright orange buffs. She didn't hear the cries from the gulls overhead as they followed the fleet for any tasty titbits coming their way. All she heard were Nanny's words rolling around in her head and, of course, she was right. When had Nanny ever been wrong? Although she'd been wrong on one thing, her eyes wandering from the sea to the shore and the display of brightly coloured shops and hotels embracing the bay like the erstwhile arms of a lover. She'd been wrong when she'd said he was mild mannered. Hadn't she seen his temper? If he'd been angry over a few chickens how might he feel when he learnt she'd made a fool of him?

She felt sick all of a sudden, sick and homesick. She walked back the way she'd come only stopping when she came to a café with a couple of empty tables outside. She didn't even know she'd taken a seat until a harried woman with a child clasped to her hip came out with a menu. Ordering a coffee she stretched her legs and let the weak March sunshine work its way over her skin and down to her bones.

'Here on holidays, are you?'

She opened her eyes to find a large mug of cappuccino in front of her and threw a smile at the woman with one child already and another on the way if the pull of her jumper was any indication.

'No, working up the road. I'm cook at the castle. I thought I'd take a walk up to the other castle?' her voice holding a question.

'Aye, Dunollie, not much to see but the gardens are nice,' she added, leaning forward. 'What's he like then?'

'What's who like?' her eyes wide.

'The lord of the manor, Lord Brayely. We don't see him much down here, keeps himself to himself up in Edinburgh with all his posh pals.'

'Really, I wouldn't know. I'm new.' She found a smile and rooting around in her jacket pulled out a handful of coins for the bill before stretching back and closing her eyes. She had another thing coming if she thought she was going to gossip about Tor.

Stopping at The Oban Fish and Chip Shop, she wandered along the esplanade and then north up to Dunollie Castle, the now derelict ruin of the MacDougall family but she didn't linger. She carried onwards and upwards, the bag of chips long forgotten her thoughts a million miles away. She had some decisions to make, big decisions and absolutely no idea how to proceed. The one thing she did know was: she couldn't carry on as she was doing. She had to leave, and as soon as possible because to stay would mean discovery. She'd been lucky, incredibly lucky no one had realised who she was but it wouldn't continue. If he found out the hard way, there'd be no telling what he'd do. He'd be angry, more than angry at being played a fool and there was no way she could ever explain why she'd done it. There was no way she was prepared to answer his questions because what could she say? She'd wanted to see if she fancied him before accepting his hand, to see if they were in any way compatible? He just wouldn't get it. He needed an heir, not some relationship. Her father had told her she wasn't important, that her opinions didn't matter. He'd never said a truer word. She was a pawn in the game of life; to be shifted from pillar to post at her father's and then her husband's bidding.

She paused for a rest, surprised to see the sun already dipping in the sky. She had no idea of the time having left both her phone and her watch back at the castle but, by the look of the clouds gathering force, it was time to head back. She found herself by a convenient tree and, sitting down on the ground, leant against the wood for a moment.

Her life in London was a complete mess. Her so called friends and the media wouldn't leave her alone. They all wanted a piece of her and if it carried on, there'd be little left. She'd only felt free in Paris and look how that had turned out, her eyes closing at the memory. Oban was like a dream, a dream where she was a working girl instead of a privileged one. But it was a mirage, a lie. She was living a lie thinking she could ever be that girl, that she could ever be Tansy Smith with her black hair and lipstick-free lips. Whilst she didn't miss the make-up or any of the other accoutrements of her former life, they were still there within grabbing distance if everything came crashing down. Home was within shouting distance and, now she knew funds were only as far away as the nearest bank, she had no reason to stay. She had no reason to stay and yet she had no intention of going. Not until she'd made her mind up about that kiss.

She woke with a start, disorientated, and it must be said, a little afraid. Where before there was light now everything around was pitch black and not only black, but cold. The temperature had dropped to what must be only a notch above freezing. She didn't know what had woken her and then she felt the first sprinkling of rain drip over her cheek and down the inside of her collar. The rain wasn't the polite London rain she was used to.

In fact, thinking about it, she couldn't remember the last time she'd been out in the rain because there was always a car or a taxi waiting on hand with someone or other with an umbrella at the ready. But here in Oban she had no umbrella. She had a far from waterproof coat and a woolly hat that even now was doing a fine job of soaking up water only to drop it down her neck, drip by drip. Standing up, she maintained contact with the bark, even as she berated herself for being so stupid as to fall asleep. There was no way she was going to be able to find her way back to Brayely Castle. In the daylight it would have been easy to mark the spot by its proximity to McCaig's Tower but now she could barely see her hand in front of her let alone a bloody tower. It was cold, wet and dark but at least the tree offered some degree of shelter...

Chapter Eight

Edinburgh was a mistake. He could run away from Brayely Castle. He could run away from her and her accusatory glare but the one thing he couldn't run away from was his thoughts.

He'd never encountered a glare like it. He couldn't quite fix on the right word but he had a pretty strong idea she loathed him; a salutary thought. He'd never been loathed before. Teased, bullied even. Ignored on occasion and perhaps hated by the odd few of his students who'd decided the best course of action for their finals was beer and guess work. But loathing was stronger than hate. Loathing was stronger than being despised, and the shiver trespassing over her skin was proof enough of her strong feelings for him. The only thing he could be pleased about was, at least she wasn't indifferent. There were some strong feelings hidden under that cool pale exterior, strong emotions worthy of his investigative powers, he thought, as his tyres snagged on the tarmac outside the front door. He'd just have to play it cool or he'd be getting a lot more than a cold stare and a shiver for his efforts.

Glancing down at his watch he noted the time with a smile. Two and a half hours as the crow flies, his fastest yet. Friday evenings with the roads clear of motorists, either drowning their sorrows in the pub or downing shots at home in front of Netflix, was obviously the way to go in future. He'd planned on getting up early and beating the Saturday morning traffic but, sitting in the bar as he half listened to his colleague discussing the new microscope the university had just ordered, he suddenly didn't see any point in staying.

He'd stood on the top step of The Balmoral Hotel, bidding him a safe journey home when he'd found himself dragged into the largest embrace. If it hadn't been for the hearty *'Mon amie,'* almost shouted into his ear before the double kiss on each cheek he'd have lifted up his clenched fists and started pummelling. There was only one man in the whole wide world who'd dare kiss him in public as his heart stumbled around in his chest trying to get a secure footing.

'*Mon amie.* Tor. *Ça fait longtemps...*'

'*Oui,* far too long, Pascal. So how is the Marquis de Sauvarin then? I hear you've become a dad since I last saw you? Congratulations.'

'*Merci.* There's Anique and then baby number two on the way. My wife…' He smiled. 'I'm still new to this wedded bliss thing but, *mon dieu*, it's the best thing I've ever done.'

'What, even better than those bowler hats you adorned each of Magdalene's four chimneys with?'

'Not a patch on being a dad. You should try it,' he added, taking his elbow and walking him back inside. 'My wife is just handing over to the babysitter; she won't leave the baby with just anybody. And then, I'd like you to meet her.'

'It would be my pleasure. You're certainly a long way from home?'

'We've been spending a few days in Stonehaven, a very special place, or for us at least. But Sarah's never been to Edinburgh so I'm showing her the sights. We head back tomorrow, first thing.'

Tor eyed his friend with affection; the Marquis de Sauvarin, the only man who'd dare kiss him. Even his father had been more of a slap on the back and double handshake kind of guy. He remembered how they'd met, although it was more of a being thrown together in desperation than actually meeting out of choice. He'd met him during Fresher's Week, all those years ago and friendships forged out of loneliness and a large dollop of homesickness were friendships forged in steel.

Accepting a pint with a smile he sat back and watched with twinkling eyes as Pascal, the most undomesticated of men, twittered around his wife until he was satisfied she had the right drink and the right chair.

'Do stop fussing, Pascal. I'm fine. More than fine now the monster's asleep.'

'Monster? '

'*Oui,* monster.' She laughed, her whole face alight with mischief.

He'd been surprised at the sight of this pretty average woman because Pascal had always had first pick and Lady Sarah, whilst cute, wasn't anything like his previous girlfriends. That is until she smiled. When she smiled it didn't matter she wasn't the prettiest in the class. It didn't matter she wasn't the tallest or the skinniest. Nothing mattered except the sweet expression on her face. Nothing mattered except the soft curve of her lips and the light streaming from her eyes. Suddenly he was reminded of Miss Smith but, by the time he'd reached for his glass, he'd lost his train of thought completely because, just like Pascal he'd fallen under her spell. Well, not just like Pascal because Lady Sarah had eyes for only one man, and sadly it wasn't him. Here was a woman he'd do anything for, anything except take Pascal on, his gaze wandering over his well-built friend cradling his beer between his hands, a self-satisfied smile stamped across his face as the baby photos were pulled out.

'She takes just after her father, little monkey.' she said, tracing a gentle finger over her chubby cheek. 'And you, Tor. Are you married?'

'Me,' he spluttered, placing his untouched beer back on the table. 'No, not exactly. There is a girl but-,' his eyes wavering between the two faces now staring at him from across the table.

'But?'

'Well, it's sort of an arranged thing.'

'An arranged thing,' her eyes wide. 'What, as in an arranged marriage?'

'Something like that, but I don't think… I'm not sure… I haven't met her yet so it will probably come to nothing.'

'I should think so too. You need to choose your own girl, Tor.' She paused, her eyes seeking out Pascal's, a frown marring her brow. 'You're not in one of those religions that go in for that kind of thing? I sort of assumed you were C of E or something but these days...'

'Actually Church of Scotland so no, it's nothing to do with religion. It's more a…' His words fell away as he tried to think what it was for? His mother would have him believe it was because he needed an heir but there were a fair few Brayely cousins knocking around so...' His train of thought was interrupted by the sound of her voice.

'A fine good looking man like you, it shouldn't be difficult.' She turned to Pascal, patting his leg. 'You need to tell him, darling. If you hadn't interfered, I could even now be married to Rupert.'

'Over my dead body!'

'Rupert? Rupert who?'

'Oh, just some fortune hunter, and anyway he's heading for divorce number three. So tell us about this girl then, what's she like?'

'As I've said, I have no idea. It's someone I knew as a child, someone I barely remember,' he mused, almost to himself, as an image of a little girl with a mass of blonde hair and legs right up to her neck came to mind. Blonde hair and long legs covered in slime. 'She was a noisy thing, that's all I remember, noisy and clumsy.'

'What's her name then? I might know her?'

'*Mon dieu,* look what you've started. You'd better tell her or we'll be here all night.'

'Titania...'

'You don't mean Titania Nettlebridge do you? You must. Surely there can't be many with that mouthful. I always felt sorry for her despite everything. There are her brothers with quite decent names and her parents had to go and lumber her with something not normally found outside of a Shakespearian play.' She burst out laughing even as she picked up her bag and pulled out a copy of Hello before flicking through the pages and marking an item with her finger. 'Here's your betrothed - Quite a looker, isn't she?'

Tor didn't want to take the magazine although he couldn't understand his reluctance. He'd been all set to meet her last week but now; now as he took the magazine from Sarah he had no interest in the woman both his mother and her parents were determined to marry him off to. No, that wasn't quite true as he caught sight of creamy pale skin and a cloud of long pale blonde hair. But it wasn't her skin or her hair that caught his attention it was her eyes, eyes he'd last seen glaring at him with that look, a look he couldn't get out of his mind. He glanced across, a puzzled look on his face before returning back to the article and scanning through the story.

'I wouldn't worry about the words, Tor. I don't know her that well but from what I can remember she's nothing like the tearaway they are portraying her as,' she whispered, taking back the magazine and rolling it up before ramming it down the side of her bag next to a dummy, a packet of baby wipes and a mangled Farley's rusk. 'The last time I saw her was at some party or other in Paris. She was working for some chef.' Her eyes met his briefly. 'There was some scandal and she had to leave in a rush. I'm not sure what she's up to now but, if I was her, I'd be in official hiding until all this nonsense blows over. She's a nice girl but I still think you should do your own choosing. Marriage is such an important step. Don't you agree, darling?' she said, clasping Pascal's hand between her palms.

'I'm beginning to think you're right.' Standing, up he pushed his untouched beer into the centre of the table and made his excuses before he could change his mind.

He nearly regretted his decision when the weather changed. He nearly stopped then. It was only the thought of a warm whisky and an even warmer bed that kept him on the road; that and the thought of having her there in the morning to cook his breakfast.

Twisting the door handle, he was surprised to feel it almost wrenched away from him by an anxious hand.

'Oh, it's you.'

'Er, yes, Toddy.' He raised his brow at the unexpected greeting only to frown as he took in the worried expression stamped on his face. 'Why? Who were you expecting?' he asked, closing the door with a quiet snap before starting to take his jacket off. 'It's a filthy night out there.'

'Aye, that it is, and Miss Smith's out in it too.'

His hand paused, his fingers tightening around the black leather collar. 'Miss Smith? It's surely a bit late for her to be out, and on a night like this?'

'It's her day off. We've been expecting her for hours, ever since the weather closed in. In fact, I should really be thinking of closing up,' he added, glancing at the grandfather clock as it started to chime the hour.

'What about Mary, what does she say? Perhaps she's an idea where she's gone?'

'I thought of that but she's not here. The mistress decided to spend the weekend with friends and took her along. Miss Campbell went up to London for the weekend. There's only me holding the fort, so to speak.'

Heaving a sigh he struggled back into his wet jacket. 'I'll go get the car if you can make a flask up, although I've no idea where to start. She's probably decided to stay with a friend and there's no way I'm going banging on every door in town.'

But that's exactly what it felt like. He headed down the hill and pulled into a parking space across from the seafront before trying every bar and late night café still open. He'd finally had success in the fish and chip shop who remembered directing a dark haired woman towards the old derelict castle and that's where he found her an hour later, curled up into a tight ball; a tight sopping wet ball.

'You little fool. What the hell do you think you're doing; trying to get pneumonia?'

He bent down and scooped her up in his arms, hardly giving her a chance to open her eyes let alone get her bearings.

'I'm too heavy.'

'Indeed.'

'Hey…'

'Well, you did ask. Now shut up like the good girl I'm quite sure you're not and let me concentrate on trying not to drop you,' as he just missed stumbling over a tree root. 'Bloody hell, and bloody women. The next cook is going to be male if I've anything to do with it; male and able to take care of himself.'

Opening her eyes all she could see was the blackness of his jacket. All she could hear was his breath as he struggled to walk down the hill with her in his arms, all the time muttering to himself at the stupidity of Sassenach cooks without a brain cell to their name. She felt the tears well up then and allowed them to fall in a steady stream down her face to mingle with the rain. He wouldn't notice and she didn't really care if he did. He didn't like her one little bit which was unfortunate as she'd quite changed her mind about him. Although, if he continued swearing at her under his breath that could all change.

When they reached the bottom, he unceremoniously opened the car door and flung her in the front.

'Here, drink this.' Turning in his seat he pushed something into her hands, only to press his warm fingers over hers. 'You're trembling.'

'It's the cold,' she said, through chattering teeth even though it wasn't. It was the sight of him and not just the sight. It was everything. In fact she couldn't remember a time she'd felt more miserable; miserable and alone. He wasn't on her side. She was a nuisance, a burden. She was someone to help only because he should. She wouldn't have been surprised if he'd just left her there as she tried and failed not to sniff.

The cold was setting up a chain of reactions but she didn't care about that. She didn't care about anything apart from the fact she'd made a mess of things yet again. Lady Tansy, the darling of the press. The poor little rich girl had yet again cocked up; the irony being of all the things she'd done in her life, this was the most important. Baking was important, as important as breathing, or at least it was to her – and she was good at it. No, she was a bloody fantastic baker but not to the man by her side. She felt the tears gather anew but she was too cold to do anything other than let them fall.

'For heaven's sake! I can't stand it when the waterworks start.'

She heard the words but the meaning didn't filter through the wall of apathy that seemed to shroud everything like a cloud. That is until she felt a handkerchief pushed roughly into her hands. Looking down, she nearly laughed at the sight of the freshly ironed white cotton so like the neat pile in the top drawer of her father's chest of drawers. At the thought of her father the tears, which up till then had only been a trickle turned into a torrent, a torrent of inconsolable drops streaming down her face with only the sound of the engine breaking the silence. She didn't realise they'd even stopped until the interior light went on and she felt his hand tilt her chin to stare into her face.

The tears dried up then. All that was left were the two of them in the car in the silence. Even the rain had stopped beating its relentless tattoo down on the soft-topped roof. She watched transfixed as he plucked the handkerchief from her stiff fingers and gently, oh so gently, wiped her tears away.

'Shush now, it's alright,' he said, speaking as if to a child.

Her eyes widened at the thought, her gaze wandering over his face. Her child. Their child. The child they'd never have. The child they could have had if she hadn't run away. If she hadn't run away she could even now be engaged… No she'd never be engaged with her father at the helm. She would have been betrothed to this surly, bad-tempered stranger with more arrogance than was good for anyone but also with the gentlest touch. Her hand curled into a fist as she remembered that meeting between him and her father because no doubt they'd have cooked something up between them in her absence.

Twisting away she fumbled for the handle only to find her hand enveloped in his.

'No, let me.' He moved her hand back onto her lap and, leaning across opened the door before walking round the bonnet and helping her out.

'Ah now, I knew you'd find her, sir. That's fine so it is. Where was she?'

'Half drowned under a tree. She'll be in need of a bath, Toddy.'

'A bath, sir?'

'Yes, a bath man. To warm up. If you could help her with a bath... There doesn't seem to be anybody else, does there, and,' his eyes now shifting across the room. 'I don't think she'll be able to manage herself.'

'Me, sir? But?'

'Yes, you.' The first tinge of impatience marking his words.

'Ach, I don't think I can.' He gulped. 'I'm a bachelor sir. I've never...'

'Get away with you. I'm only asking you to run the thing and get the towels...' He paused, and they both stared towards the stairs, the bottom stair to be exact; the bottom stair where he'd propped her up only seconds before. But now she wasn't so much propped as stretched out very much in the style of a rag doll. They eyed each other for a moment before he finally spoke.

'She'll get her death if she doesn't...' He stood up with a sigh, grasping his old friend's arm with a gentle squeeze. 'Right, together then. No arguments and then some soup.'

'Certainly, sir, and there's a nice raised pie in the larder...'

'Not for me Toddy. For her.' His eyes now back on the stairs. 'All I need is in the lounge or, to be exact, in the whisky decanter in the lounge and you can join me. You know I hate drinking on my own.'

Later, much later, a couple of drams of Oban's very own single malt later, he sat in front of the fire, his feet resting on the antique barley twist fender just like his father and grandfather before him. The castle might boast twelve bathrooms and the new addition of underfloor heating but there was still very little he was allowed to do to change the fabric of the building. They tried to economise in other ways but there was no way he would ever skimp on warmth. The coal scuttles were always heaving as were the log baskets. They didn't heat every room just the ones in constant use and all of the servants' quarters, of course. A happy servant was a warm one, his brow wrinkling at the thought. He viewed them more as friends, friends with financial benefits as opposed to any other sort, although he'd quite like to think about the other sort of 'benefit' where Lady Titania Smith-Nettlebridge was concerned.

He ground his teeth before raising the vintage thistle patterned glass to his lips, his eyes relishing the way the firelight reflected and bounced off the finely etched surface. Miss Smith-Nettlebridge was someone he had spent the last hour trying not to think about. Up close and personal, her skin was even paler than he'd ever imagined, not that he'd seen much of it.

They'd decided, as they both had reputations to uphold, that the best course of action was to dunk her in the hot water fully clothed, apart from her socks and her boots. She had pretty feet, he remembered, the smooth fiery liquid tracing its way down his throat. Long slender feet with simple square cut toenails. He'd been expecting varnish. No, that wasn't quite true, as he raised the glass to his mouth, letting the cold glass press against his bottom lip. He hadn't been expecting anything because he'd turned off all thought and all emotion when they'd entered the bathroom. But he had been surprised all the same. There wasn't a mark on her; no tattoos, toe rings or ankle bracelets for that matter. He thought they all went in for that sort of thing these days.

He eyed the rest of the whisky before heaving a sigh of regret. He had work to do tomorrow and a hangover wasn't part of the plan. In fact, any trace of a hangover and he'd throw up. The seas around the Firth of Lorn were well known for their inclemency and he still had samples to collect from the most isolated island of all.

Chapter Nine

'I'll have to leave, there's no two ways...' she mumbled, dragging the sharp teeth of her comb through her hair with a grimace before working a neat plait with deft fingers. *'I love it here. I love the silence. I love the scenery and even the early starts.'*

She turned and stared out of the window, feasting her gaze on the still dark night as she wondered where she should go. She could go back to London and back to her previous life of parties and trips to Harrods and Harvey Nicks with her mother, but the glitz and glamour had dimmed somewhat. The glitz and glamour hadn't so much dimmed as been smashed by a pair of the bluest eyes and a pair of the strongest hands.

She didn't want to go back. She didn't want to leave Scotland. No, that wasn't quite true. She didn't want to leave him. Pulling on her felt slippers with the pretty diamante flowers, she hurried out of the room and traipsed down the stairs with a light foot. She had breakfast to cook and an apology to make. After that, and only after, would she think about tomorrow and what the hell she was going to do with the next fifty years or so.

Entering the kitchen, she wondered what it was about him that ticked all her boxes because charming he wasn't. He was probably the most arrogant, bad tempered, rude man she'd ever met. Opening the fridge to take out the milk, she decided there was no probably about it. She'd focus on his bad points and forget the rest as she tried to close her mind to the memory of his touch and the feel of his lips roaming across her skin.

Stoking the Aga took seconds. The kettle was always the first job, the kettle set to boil while she sorted out the chickens. But today, with the mistress and most of the staff away she had more than enough eggs to be going on with. She'd still need to visit the coop but later would do.

She set the teapot on the table and, cradling her mug, took it outside to spend precious minutes she couldn't really afford just staring out on to the shadowy terrace. She still hadn't decided what to do, but as Nanny always said

Do nothing and something will happen…

'Morning. Any tea in the pot?'

She nearly dropped her mug. If she hadn't been resting it on her thigh there would have been broken crockery to pick up and not just the spreading stain where she'd tipped tea over her leg.

'Now look what you've made me do.'

'Excuse me?'

But instead of replying, she stood up only to find his hand on her shoulder pushing her back onto the bench.

'No, you stay where you are, Miss Smith. I'll get it and I'll fetch you a top-up too,' he added, taking her mug from her hand and walking back inside.

'Of all the overbearing bossy...'

'You said something?'

She blushed, struggling to avoid his gaze but meeting his eyes all the same. The blush deepened as she remembered waking up in bed in a towel and nothing else. She had no idea how she'd got there, no idea at all. She had no idea, only suspicions.

'Just talking to myself,' she finally managed; taking the mug he was holding.

'That's alright then.'

She raised an eyebrow, waiting for him to continue.

'Well, I talk to myself all the time. Sometimes it's the best sense I can get all week.' He sat down beside her, stretching out his legs with a sigh. 'Try making sense out of a pile of spotty teenagers scarcely old enough to tie up their shoelaces let alone be let loose in the big wicked city?'

'Big wicked city?'

'Edinburgh. That's where I teach, when I can't avoid not to, that is.' He tilted his head back, his eyes closed to the first shafts of light starting to turn the sky from black to navy.'

'But, I don't understand? Why do you have to teach when you have all this?' She threw out a hand, sweeping it towards the dark twisted branches now just visible in the distance. 'Surely you can't need the money?'

'Oh can't I, little miss nosy? There's more to life than money you know.' He shifted and now instead of his neck she was staring into his eyes, eyes as black as his stare as he scrolled over her face with the precision of an artist about to embark on a masterpiece. His hand raised and, with a slight twist, he grabbed the end of her plait before giving it a sharp tweak.

'Teaching comes with the territory. If I want to be able to use the university's resources to further my studies I need to give something back, and teaching the odd student is the only way. I don't have a full time post now, just the odd lecture… Tell me, why would someone with such pretty hair decide to dye it such an ugly colour?'

'Tell me,' she echoed. 'How can someone with all the opportunities you've had turn out to be so bloody objectionable?' She stood up, and pulling her hair out of his grasp headed back into the kitchen. 'I'm employed to cook, Lord Brayely, and I'll thank you to keep any personal comments you may have to yourself.'

Her back turned she ignored his quiet footsteps as he made his way to the sink and painstakingly washed his mug before leaving it upside down on the draining board. She didn't care if he was trying to be helpful. She didn't care if, at some time in his life, somebody had actually taught him how to do the dishes. She didn't care that his eyes were on her every movement as she went back and forth to the larder before cracking eggs in the heavy iron skillet.

She didn't care, and yet she cared desperately.

'I'll have mine in the kitchen, and make that three eggs. I'll probably be back late.'

Slapping down a loaf on the cutting board she started to slice bread for toasting only to find the knife gently removed from her grasp.

'I'll do that while you watch the eggs. I don't have much time before I leave.'

'If you'd let me know yesterday,' she grumbled, adding a few chopped mushrooms to the pan.

'And when would I have done that exactly? It's not as if you were in any fit state to be listening to my plans for the day.'

She set his breakfast down at the far end before refilling the teapot.

'I meant to thank you for, for…'

'For finding you? Don't mention it, all part and parcel of being lord of the manor,' he added, smoothing marmalade on his toast before taking a hearty bite. 'There won't be much cooking to do today with ma away. In fact, you might as well take the day off. Toddy is used to looking after himself. He'll probably want to spend the day with his sister in town, come to think of it.'

'Thank you.' She sat down opposite, pouring herself a mug from the pot without a second thought. 'Can I ask you a question without you snapping my head off?' she said, raising her head to meet his steady gaze.

'As long as you're quick. For some reason, I'm in a good mood, so ask away, Miss Smith and I promise I won't snap, unless it's personal that is? Then chances are, I may er 'snap' as you call it,' he added on a wink.

'As if! No, it's about Mr Todd. Why do you…?

'Why do I what, call him Toddy?' He placed his knife and fork tidily in the centre of his plate before pushing his mug in the direction of the teapot. 'That's what I've always called him. He's been here a long time, you know. I was only a teenager when he arrived and he took me under his wing. We're friends more than anything, despite me paying his wages. Two lonely souls trying to make their way...'

She raised her eyebrows. 'He does seem a little serious. Such a nice man and he never married?'

'Not all men want marriage, Tansy.' He gave her a sharp look, before continuing. 'I can see where you're coming from with Toddy; he'd have made a wonderful father. I think there was someone, a girl in Lewis, but for some reason it didn't work out. He's never said anything, we don't have that sort of relationship but I seem to remember my father let something slip about some housemaid or other. She'd probably have made his life a misery. That's what women do. They attract you with their pretty face and womanly wiles, reeling you in like a fish on a hook before slitting your underbelly and spilling out your guts.'

She ignored his comment. She was enjoying sitting there having a conversation of sorts, even if it was only about the butler. But one wrong word or look and he'd be biting her head off.

He was waiting for her reaction, she just knew he was but she wasn't going to give him the satisfaction of rising to his bait even if it killed her. Instead, she focussed on the first part of his answer even if the questions she really wanted to ask tumbled around her head like dust balls in the desert. Who or what had made him so sceptical about life and about love in particular? He'd obviously been hurt at the hand of a woman and she now couldn't stop thinking about what had happened. Had he been dumped, was that it? Or was it something worse, much worse? Maybe he'd been young and impressionable although, shooting him a look, she couldn't imagine he'd ever had that quality laid at his feet. He was the most put together man she'd ever met. He was a man who knew where he was going and how he was going to get there, not someone like her who lurched from one crisis to the next.

Picking up her mug she finally managed to ask. 'Where's Lewis, it's one of the islands, isn't it?'

'Yep, but the Outer Hebrides.'

'I'm planning on visiting some of the islands if I get the chance.'

'Oh, you'll have time. You can come with me today, that is, if you can bear the company of an overbearing bossy...'

'I didn't mean…'

'Yes you did, and you're probably right, come to that.' He rested his elbows on the table and stared at her over the top of his mug. 'Tell you what, as an apology, I'll treat you to an early lunch on Seil and then, if you're feeling brave, you can accompany me over to Belnahua. It'll be by boat, mind. I hope you're not prone to seasickness?'

'Me, I've a cast iron stomach,' she quipped back, the beginning of a smile lurking behind her mock serious face. 'What do I need to bring?'

'Just yourself and perhaps a flask of tea. Belnahua is uninhabited so there won't be some café to pop into for a cream cake, or even a loo, come to that.'

'I'll have you know I've got my gold D of E!'

'Really? You do surprise me.' His head tilted so he could look at her pink slippers glittering in the weak Scottish sun.

'I thought you were going to stop with the snarky remarks already?'

'No.' He stood up from the table and started gathering together his dishes. 'What I said was I'd apologise for commenting on your hair, although the comment still stands.' He ended, pulling the door open only to pause, his hand high up on the jamb. 'Wrap up warm. Belnahua is no trek with the promise of a warm bed at the end. It's bleak, cold, uninhabited and potentially dangerous.'

'So tell me about this island then. Bell...'
'Belnahua?'
They were sitting side by side in The Oyster Bar, their eyes drawn like magnets to the wonderful view of the other islands. Tor had promised her lunch but she hadn't quite bargained for the homemade thick vegetable soup followed by crispy mouth-watering haddock wrapped in the best batter she'd ever tasted. Now, with mugs of rich dark coffee before them while they waited for the boat he'd hired to be brought around to the shoreline, she asked the first in a raft of questions.
'Belnahua, that's it. It sounds romantic.'
'Romantic is it?' He flung his head back and laughed, the sound turning the heads of the locals propping up the bar. 'It's far from romantic, more like tragic. It's been uninhabited since the war; the First World War when all the men went off to fight and probably never to return. Any romance, as you put it, would have died then. All that's left is a pile of broken down slate to match the broken down houses and a few wild animals.
'Wild animals?' She questioned with a frown. 'What kind of wild animals?'

'Oh, nothing to worry your pretty little head about. A few gulls and maybe a wolf or two. No lions, tigers or bears.'

'Wolf...' She started to ask only to look up and see his smug expression. Promptly shutting her mouth, she decided there was no point in asking anything else, not if he was going to tease her. Okay, so she wasn't the brightest light on the Christmas tree but that didn't give him the right to *take the Mickey*. The remaining questions queuing up on her tongue shrivelled to nothing. Questions like why was he visiting if there was nothing to see? She'd thought they'd got past the animosity of earlier. She'd thought they'd become, if not friends, then friendly.

The trip across to Seil and that cute little humpbacked bridge linking the island to the mainland was so scenic with the first of the spring flowers just starting to show their heads out of the cold bare soil. They'd even managed to share a few laughs about yesterday and how Mr Todd, confirmed bachelor that he was, had nearly died at having to help him lift her into bed and then spoon soup into her. She didn't remember any of it but had sighed a silent sigh of relief at the thought of there being the two of them present. She wasn't a prude. Recent events of having most of her assets displayed on the front page of most of the daily newspapers had drummed out any last dregs of prudish behaviour, but she was glad all the same.

However, now she felt like tipping the remains of her coffee all over his head and not just the coffee, her fingers itching to curl them around the nearly full water jug; the sanctimonious little prig.

'I'm sorry, I shouldn't tease, Tansy…' he said, grabbing her hand and unfurling her fingers before placing them flat on the table. 'I don't know what it is about you but you bring out the worst in me,' his hand covering hers. 'Was it the coffee I was nearly wearing or the contents of the jug?'

'Both!' She stood up, and picking up her rucksack flung it across her narrow shoulders. 'Hadn't we better be going if you're going to do whatever it is you have to?'

'Good idea.'

'When you said bleak, I didn't quite realise just how bleak.'

They'd anchored offshore and used a rubber dinghy to make their way to the beach, although it wasn't like any beach she'd ever been to. Instead of sand, there were piles and piles of deep grey slate; piles of the slipperiest deep grey slate.

'It's a good job I've done a fair bit of ice-skating in my time.'

'Really, where did you..?'

'Oh, Central Park. My parents used to take us…'

'Us?' he asked, grabbing her hand to help her up the steep incline that would take them onto the overgrown path.

'I think I told you I have two brothers?'

'That must have cost a fair bit. What does your father do exactly?'

Oh God, what was she going to reply to that? She couldn't think of anything to say other than the truth and the truth would never do, hysterical laughter building up in the back of her throat.

My dad, what does he do? He doesn't do anything; he doesn't have to, what with being the second largest landowner in Surrey, in addition to having homes in both Belgravia and Provence. He is in the House of Lords though. Does that count?

She stumbled and, if it hadn't been for his arm she'd have landed flat on her face.

'Are you alright?'

He'd placed his other hand around her, smoothing her hair back under the black beanie she'd had the foresightedness to wear at the last minute.

Was she alright, her eyes meeting his in an echo of the night she'd helped him with his bow tie? Oh, she wasn't injured or anything. Her arm ached a little from where he'd had to wrench her back to standing but she could hardly feel it above the thumping of her heart. Thump, thump, thump, it pounded in her ears, louder than the seagulls overhead or the waves crashing against the shore behind them in a symphony of sound. She opened her mouth to speak, to tell him she was fine but she wasn't fine. She was as far from fine as it was possible to be. She moistened her lips in preparation to speak the words and now he wasn't watching her, his attention taken up with her mouth, her skin, her…

She didn't know which one moved first, probably her but whatever. Rucksacks crashed onto shale as lips met lips and clocks stopped ticking. The wind stilled, the birds stopped flapping and Poseidon halted the sea on its relentless quest.

There was complete silence. Even the beat of her heart stopped as skin met skin, only to start thrashing around in her chest as his hand drew her in ever closer. He was devouring her. There was nothing she wanted more than to be devoured.

Slowly, imperceptibly, irrevocably, the outside world peeked through the fugue. The waves made up for lost time. The seagulls screeched and squawked while the wind decided to join in the party by trying to blow them off their feet. There was nothing she wanted more than to continue but not here on a bed of long forgotten broken shale.

He hadn't been wrong about her as she reeled in her senses and started the long hard process of lip reclamation. She liked her creature comforts and, whilst she had a gold D of E medal gently rusting in the bottom of her jewellery box, it was the hardest thing she'd ever done.

Finally the last infinitesimal second of breath, of touch, of sensation was over. Air was drawn into desperate lungs and common sense decided it was time to interrupt their happy interlude – was it happy?

She was standing in the circle of his arms, his forehead dipped to meet hers and she didn't even like him more than that. Tor was the rudest, bossiest, most overbearing man. A man she'd just discovered she'd given her heart to along with that kiss; her heart and her soul.

And what was she to him? Nothing. Less than nothing. A passing fancy, no more. He hadn't a good word to say about her apart from comments about her cooking. He even hated her hair but then... She hated her hair so that didn't mean much.

She eased away, or at least as far away as his hands would let her because it seemed he wasn't letting go of her any time soon.

'Are you alright?' he repeated, smoothing the pads of both thumbs along her cheeks. 'I didn't mean for that to happen.'

No, I'm sure you didn't, the words echoing inside her head as she struggled to turn thoughts into actions. Easing back she shook her head briefly still unable to come up with any words that would be deemed appropriate, words that wouldn't put her in the wrong because of course he'd blame her. Everyone always blamed the girl. It had happened before and now it would happen again. Well, he couldn't pull that little trick on her, she wouldn't let him. She'd done nothing. She'd said nothing. She was wearing jeans, for God's sake, her oldest, scruffiest jeans. It wasn't her fault but she'd be to blame just like she'd been to blame in Paris. Louis's wife had blamed her, only her, when she'd arrived home and found them together because there was no way her beloved husband would ever look at another woman unless she'd thrown herself at him.

She paused, her eyes on the shingle bank ahead; her mind seeing nothing but Paris.

'I'm fine.'

There, the words were out, lies both of them but they'd have to do. She wasn't fine, she'd never be fine again but, as it was all her fault, the words were immaterial. Reaching down she picked up her rucksack and forged ahead towards what looked like the first in a line of derelict cottages. She could hear him sigh somewhere over her left shoulder but decided to ignore him. Instead, placing her bag on a convenient rock she rooted in the front pocket before pulling out her phone.

'I doubt very much you'll get a signal,' he quipped, his voice laced with sarcasm and something else she couldn't quite identify. Embarrassment? Confusion? Disgust at snogging the hired help for a second time?

'Really?' Head bowed she didn't see his expression; if she had she might have added desire to the list. But she was too engrossed in trying to fake interest in her messages to notice. All she wanted was to fling herself into his arms and continue where they'd left off, which would never do. However, there was something…

'Say cheese.' She looked up, phone raised and clicked. She might not have the man, even now looking increasingly annoyed, but at least she'd have him forever captured as she'd best remember him; windswept, arrogant and sexy as hell with just a hint of redness where her lips had stamped their mark of passion for eternity.

'Hey!'

'What? I'll delete it if you like?' she said, scrolling back to the photo. 'It wouldn't have harmed you to smile.'

'I smile when there's something to smile at.'

'Ever the charmer.' She pulled back the sleeve of her jacket and looked at her watch. 'Hadn't you'd better start doing whatever it is you're meant to be doing? I'm going to wander around the ruins, but I won't go far in case there are any wolves about,' she added, a brief smile on her lips. They both knew there was only one wolf on Belnahua, a wolf more dangerous than any four legged variety.

She started fiddling around with her phone again, well aware she was being studied but to hell with him. He'd had his fun. He was probably laughing to himself at how easy she'd been. Well, bully for him. She wasn't going to give him the satisfaction of showing her feelings. He could think what he wanted. As soon as Lady Brayely came back, she'd make up some excuse or other and… And that was the problem. She had no idea what came next.

She turned and watched as he stalked over to the other side of the island, his plain black bag dangling from his fingers. She'd fallen in love with the man she was meant to be betrothed to. In itself it sounded the perfect solution to all her problems apart from one little hiccup. He didn't love her, but more than that. He didn't respect her and, if and when he found out the trick she'd played on him... Well, she dreaded to think what would happen.

Squeezing her eyes she resisted the temptation to follow, suddenly aware of the silence, a silence only broken by the odd cry from the gulls circling overhead. Instead of following, she turned back towards the stream of tumbledown cottages stretched out before her. She'd do what she'd intended and have a look around. It would be out of the biting wind but, more importantly, it would help keep her mind off her troubles.

The first cottage wasn't really a cottage just three walls and an old warped door swinging back and forward in the breeze; beckoning, enticing, tempting. There was no point in stopping but still she lingered, her gaze drawn to the fireplace and the black embers still visible even after all this time. What was it he'd said again; deserted since the war when they'd closed down operations and flooded both quarries, turning them into lochs. All those families having to leave their homes, their husbands dragged off to fight in a war they probably knew little about.

She felt her eyes prick but instead of giving way to tears, tears that would only in part be for the shadows hovering between the lichen covered bricks, she pulled the door closed and walked on to the next cottage.

This had fared better with the walls and most of the windows intact. There was even a roof of sorts; a slate roof. Pushing the door open revealed a room with an open fireplace carved into stone and an old cooking pot still hanging over the hearth. Apart from an old rickety cupboard listing against one wall, there was little else. Of the occupants who'd lived, loved and presumably died here, there was little trace.

Slate workers, she remembered as she brushed a gentle finger over the rim of the pot. Slate workers and their families cut off and isolated for months on end while the Scottish winter weather did its worst. There'd have been no electricity. No running water. No amenities. There'd have been nothing to dispel the bare bleakness of the place, her foot dragging against the bare earth floor bereft of any flooring or matting. Where had they slept? Where had they eaten? She couldn't begin to imagine the life they'd led, working long hours in the quarries only to return in near darkness to spend their time reading and sewing by candlelight. Would there have been a school? There'd have been children but… She knew so little about what it must have been like except that it would have been hard.

She closed the door on all the forgotten memories and wandered outside, her eyes now on the horizon. She could live here like that if she had the right man by her side. Her needs, after all, weren't that extravagant, her eyes tracing down to her boots, her hiking boots she'd bought on a whim last time she'd been in Bond Street. She had no idea how much they'd cost. All she knew was she'd been invited to a weekend party in the country and they'd matched her Burberry, her new Burberry. The Burberry she'd decided to leave at home. She could get away with decent boots because shoes were important but her wax jacket had gone the same way as her Prada sunglasses and the Bulgari diamond earrings she'd worn since her eighteenth birthday. She'd even left her watch at home, instead making do with a cheap digital she'd picked up in the train station. It was fine, more than fine, as she stared down at the fluorescent pink strap. She liked pink. The only thing that wasn't fine was the time.

Tor had said he wouldn't be long. In fact he'd made a point of telling her not to wander far because he wanted to get back before dark. So where the hell was he then, her attention drawn to the sun's rapid descent towards the waters beyond her vision? Throwing her bag across her shoulders she raced down the path and across the overgrown track, thankful at least he'd left a trail of flattened bracken and gorse as easy to follow as any breadcrumbs.

It didn't take her long to find herself on the other side of the island but there was still no sign of him. Shouting his name into the wind her eyes fixed on the sea and their boat gently bobbing on its anchor. She'd imagined for a second he'd been so fed up that he'd decided to desert her. She could imagine many things of him but not that.

She remembered he'd said something about collecting samples as she changed direction and headed away from the beach, her eyes now scanning backwards and forwards until she found what she was looking for. Running now, running and tripping over the shale bed, she galloped across to the centre of the island as she remembered he'd mentioned the rock on the rim of the lochs; lochs forged from the devastation wreaked by centuries of mining. He'd even suggested a dip on a laugh, his gaze running the length of her body; a dip in zero degree waters. He was in for a rude shock if he thought she was stripping off anywhere near him, wind or no wind.

If it hadn't been for his red scarf she'd never have found him; that was her second thought. Her first thought wasn't really a thought at all just a stream of tears at the relief of finding what she was beginning to think she'd lost; lost before they'd even had a chance to begin. She didn't concentrate too much on where her chaotic thoughts were taking her; thoughts, selfish thoughts like just how long she'd have survived on a flask of coffee and a pack of chocolate digestives? There was no water on the island, no drinking water that is, her eyes veering across the eerie surface of the drowned mine. They used to gather rain water in buckets and she hadn't even seen a bucket, only that black pot and its family of bone crunching spiders.

'Hey, asleep on the job...'

She reached him and the words clogged in the back of her throat because, whilst it might look like he was asleep stretched out on the long grass, the darkening bruise on his forehead told a different story. She wasn't alone as she'd feared. He hadn't deserted her but he might as well have.

'Tor, Tor wake up,' her cries increasingly frantic, her hand gentle and then less gentle, moulding to his shoulder pressing, pummelling before finally dropping to her side. He was dead to the world if not actually dead, her eyes now in a frenzy as she watched his chest heave up and down with an annoying regularity. If he was putting it on, she'd bloody kill him.

But after another ten minutes she finally realised the horrible truth. She was alone on Belnahua, a deserted island with an unconscious man. A man who was in need of first-aid and she didn't have a clue where to start. The one thing she did know was the temperature; never much above freezing was dropping. The temperature was dropping and the little light left was disappearing to reveal a cloudless star-filled night sky.

Chapter Ten

'What the…'

'About bloody time too!'

Resting back on her heels as he struggled to sitting, she'd have felt scared at the sight of his glare if she hadn't felt pure unadulterated relief at the sight of him doing anything other than snoring for the last thirty minutes. He was angry, blisteringly angry but angry was better than unconscious any day. Okay, so they were still stranded and he still didn't look in anyway fit to trek down the hill over all that shale but at least he wasn't dead. He was far from dead, her eyes pinned to his face, his dripping wet face where she'd thrown ice cold water from the loch in a last ditch attempt to wake him up.

'I thought you were dead,' she said, fumbling to replace the top on the flask.

'Me, dead? It would take more than what Belnahua has to throw at me for that,' he mumbled back, dragging the ends of his scarf over his face.

He still didn't look right. His eyes in the dim light had that glazed look as if he was trying to focus. She'd expected him to rant and rave but, apart from his initial outburst, he'd flopped back down, his head in his hands.

She moved closer until she was within touching distance and, reaching out a hand, placed it over his.

'Are you alright?' Her words mirroring his of earlier.

'I'm not sure,' he muttered, his fingers reaching up to feel the egg on his head. 'I'm not sure I can walk either, I must have twisted my ankle when I tripped, or at least I think that's what must have happened. I can't really remember…' His look dazed. 'If we don't move we'll freeze.' He shifted, his face dragging into a grimace. 'I should never have brought you…'

'And what would have happened if you hadn't? Just like a man not to think things through properly,' she added, picking up her rucksack where she'd placed it next to his. 'I'm taking you down that hill. There's a cottage of sorts, and we have chocolate biscuits,' she wheedled.

'Well then, that's alright isn't it? We're stuck in the middle of nowhere in freezing temperatures, with no light, no heat and no water but we do have biscuits, and chocolate at that.'

'I have light,' she replied, pulling out her keys and pressing a button, a miniscule torch emitting about as much light as a glow-worm.

'Yeah, right!'

'I also have paracetamol and a picnic blanket but if you're not interested…?'

The walk down the hill was one she never wanted to repeat. They somehow stumbled and shuffled over the rough terrain his arm wrapped around her shoulder as she half pushed, half pulled and finally dragged him, all by the light of her torch because that's all they had.

His mood, dark before, was positively morose when she finally managed to propel him into the cottage and sink him to the ground. Shining the torch up into his face she was shocked to see grey skin where before there'd been rude health.

She quickly unpacked both rucksacks before fashioning a pillow, of sorts, from the two empty bags and placing it under his head. That was about all she could do, apart from covering him with the blanket and helping him down a couple of tablets. She'd decided to leave his boot on. He'd obviously damaged his ankle being as it was swollen to balloon proportions but it would be suicide to try and attempt walking across the slate bed in the morning in socks. She'd untied his laces and would have liked to have elevated his leg if there'd been anything to elevate it on but there was nothing…

By now it was six o'clock but it felt a lot later. It was pitch black and she was tired, hungry and afraid. He'd fallen back to sleep again but, touching his hand, he was cold, so cold and it wasn't as if she could click a switch to turn up the heating. If she'd seen any wood on the island she'd have attempted to light a fire but there was nothing to burn. Cramming her mouth full of biscuits she took a sip of coffee but only a sip. They'd need it in the morning. He'd need it, if only to swallow more painkillers.

Sitting beside him, his hand in hers she thought back to earlier and the romanticism she'd felt at the thought of living the puritanical life of an islander with a good man at her side. It wasn't romantic, a solitary tear tracing its way down her cheek. It wasn't heart-warming and life fulfilling. It was bloody awful, her gaze now on the other side of the room where the pot was, the big black pot full of the biggest blackest spider. Even as she imagined it, she heard the sound of something scuttling across the floor. Scooting beside him she shifted a little of the rucksack from under his head before squashing up next to him under the plaid rug. The best thing, the only thing for it was sleep. Asleep she could get through the night. Awake - no chance.

She was asleep. She was dreaming. She was dreaming of him again. Oh, it wasn't the first time. She'd been dreaming about him for quite a while now, long before she'd even met him. It was only recently she'd finally been able to put a face to the lips, the arms, the skin, the feel. Ever since her parents had reminded her of his existence he'd featured as the sole dream inhabitant. She'd never been a great one for dreaming. Even after the incident with Louis she hadn't taken the bedroom scene into her subconscious to dwell on. So why now did she wake up each morning with a lingering sense of happiness just out of range? She didn't remember the dreams. She didn't remember anything other than they featured him in a range of guises and she'd felt happy.
But life has a way of intruding on dreams. We sleep, we dream, we wake and wake she did only to find her dream, for once, wasn't a dream.
Somehow during the night the earth had shifted, or she'd shifted. Whatever the reason, instead of lying tucked under his arm snuggling up for warmth she was now lying on top of him, her head tucked into his neck, her

knees bent up around his waist as if she was holding on for dear life. She could feel his breath on her cheek just as she could feel his heartbeat thumping next to her through the thickness of their jackets. But it wasn't just her that must have moved as she felt his arms wrapped around her back, his hands pressing her even closer and not just pressing as she sensed a shift. He was awake and she was trapped.

She didn't know what to feel; happy or sad. But she certainly wasn't upset about this turn of events, just a little worried as to what would happen next.

'If you could just move your leg a couple of centimetres to the right,' his breath coming out in a gasp and she finally realised just where her knee was resting.

'Oh, sorry…' she stuttered. 'I must have… It must have been cold,' she finally managed to squeak into his neck.

'Very cold, but the temperature does appear to be hotting up,' he added, raising his arm and lifting her head up, his gaze running over her face with a smile. 'Did I thank you for yesterday, or was I a beast?'

'More like a bear with a sore head. How is it today?' she said, trying and failing to sit up as the hand across her back turned to a ribbon of steel.

'I think I'll live, but only if I have a good woman to look after me. Are you a good woman, Tansy?'

'No, probably not.'

'Shame, well I'll just have to make do with a bad one then.' His lips finally doing what she'd been hoping they'd do all along.

She forgot she was lying on a hard floor in the middle of nowhere with no creature comforts like a feather bed or even a comb. She forgot she hadn't cleaned her teeth or washed her face. She forgot everything except his mouth on hers, his teeth snagging at her lower lip exploring, teasing, pulling before finally descending inside to plunder without apology. She was his completely, utterly, undoubtedly and he was staking his claim. His hand was on her face, her neck, her back before wandering through all the layers and lighting a trail of fire across her skin, despite the cool morning air inveigling its presence. She was lost then; lost but for the very first time in her life not alone as she joined him kiss for kiss, her knees pressing against his body, ever closer, ever more daring…

She hadn't wanted to start. Now she didn't want it to end but end it did slowly, reluctantly, fatefully his hand still lingering on her breast.

'You'd better stop me, because I don't seem to be able to stop myself where you're concerned,' he sighed, placing one last kiss against her lips before removing his hand and helping her to pull her jumper back in place.

'You didn't have to stop...' She blushed, but managed to keep hold of his gaze all the same as she stood up and dragged her coat back in place.

'Oh didn't I? So you'd be happy for me to take you on a dirt bed, would you? Like some feudal war lord? I think I can manage something a little more romantic or...' He paused, his gaze raking her from head to foot. 'Or is that what you're used to, Tansy? Is this the real Tansy? Not the shy, little girl that gets lost in the hills but a fully-fledged woman who's happy for a bit of rough? Who's happy to take whatever she can get from whoever's available even if she doesn't like them more than that. You don't like me very much, do you?' His voice harsh.

She stared down at him, her face going from red to pale in an instant. She didn't like him very much. No. She loved him with all her being and that's what she thought she'd been telling him with, if not her words then her lips. He obviously hadn't got the message and she was blowed if she was going to translate.

'No, I don't like you more than that,' a crack in her voice as she struggled to keep tears at bay. He didn't like tears but if he shouted at her again, she very much doubted she could hold them back.

Their journey back was a silent one, silent apart from his apology. Oh, he wasn't apologising for calling her a tart in all but name. He was apologising for having to place his arm on her shoulder as his ankle was still unsteady, still hurting. He was apologising for having to rely on someone, anyone other than himself. He was apologising for everything and anything except what he should have been apologising for. She hadn't deserved his treatment of her but there it was. She wasn't going to get even a stray sorry for that.

They managed between them to row the dinghy back to the boat and, if his entry across the gunnel wasn't perfect at least they were on board after a fashion and his hands were able to work the engine. By the time they'd reached the shore his face was set into a permanent frown. He was angry, furiously angry with her. So angry he'd stopped speaking all together but - if looks could kill she'd be at the bottom of the ocean now swimming with the fishes.

She remained silent, her face turned away from his stony glares. She'd offered herself to him on a platter and he'd thrown it back in her face. So what if she'd lied and said she didn't like him? After all, he wasn't the most likeable of men. Did he honestly think she enjoyed being shouted at even if she'd been in the wrong, yet again? The chickens, the kiss. He'd even blame her for his accident if he could.

His mood didn't improve when he realised there was no way he was going to be able to drive.

'But you're not insured,' the first words he'd uttered in over an hour.

'Yes I am,' she said. 'I'm insured to drive any vehicle' - Including an HGV - but she wasn't going to tell him driving was a hobby. More than a hobby, more like an obsession. She wasn't going to tell him both Hamilton and Isaac were car obsessed and that they'd dragged her around all the motor shows. She also wasn't going to tell him she had her pilot's licence. Information like that was on a need to know basis and, after the way he'd just treated her, he needed to know as little as possible.

'You enjoy driving?' were the next words out of his mouth, and only uttered as she turned into the driveway of Brayely Castle.

'Yes,' the only word out of hers as she pulled to a stop, the smile on her face for Mr Todd waiting on the top step. Hopping out and collecting her bag from the backseat her voice was deliberately cheerful even though her heart was now rattling around her chest like a bag of broken china. 'Lord Brayely has had a

bit of an accident if you could help him, please.
'

'Right you are. Her ladyship is back. She'd like pork chops for supper so I took the liberty of calling the butcher.'

She placed a hand on his shoulder with a smile. 'Thank you. I'll make extra for the staff so and perhaps one of my fruit pies?'

Saturday afternoon came and went with no more disturbances on the Tor front. It was Saturday evening when she next heard his name mentioned, although just because no one had mentioned him didn't mean she hadn't thought about him with every waking breath. She was a fool, more than a fool to let it get this far. She was a fool not to have taken it further, as she kneaded and pummelled the latest batch of dough before placing it in the prepared loaf tin and coating it with poppy seeds.

She was getting into the swing of this cooking lark having rediscovered the trick; preparation, preparation, preparation so that when it was actually time to do any cooking everything was to hand. She had the bacon sliced for breakfast and the plumpest pork sausages. She was a great believer in a hearty Sunday morning breakfast as there was nothing worse than sitting in a cold church with only hunger for company. She wasn't sure what Lady Brayely thought about baked beans but tomorrow morning she was about to find out.

Mary wandered in with her ladyship's cup and saucer all set for a chat.

'Hot chocolate, Mary, and a slice of apple tart?'

'Yum, but only if you'll join me? Her ladyship is in a right ole mood this evening.'

'Oh? What's got up her goat then?' she said, putting hot milk in the pan to boil. She didn't do instant hot chocolate. Hot chocolate was an art she'd learnt in France and, whilst it was fiddly the final result topped with hand-whipped cream and a sprinkling of dark chocolate shavings held little resemblance to the 'just add hot water' varieties sold across the land.

'That son of hers.'

'What's he been doing to upset her now?' she said faintly, adding a little cold milk to cream the cocoa powder in the bottom of the mugs.

'She's desperate for him to settle down. To be honest, I think she'd be happy for him to marry anyone, as long as it's not Cassandra.'

'Why's that?' She started pouring the hot milk, beating with a little hand whisk until all the lumps disappeared before topping with cream, lots of cream followed by lots of chocolate.

'That looks amazing,' Mary said, pulling the mug towards her and taking a small sip, a smile breaking across her face. She threw her a quick glance before continuing. 'I think it's because of his wife.'

'His wife? I didn't know he was married.' She reached for a cloth and wiped the table where she'd just spilt the top off her chocolate.

'Didn't you?' Mary smiled again, but this time not with her lips, her eyes twinkling amusement. 'It was when he was in college - some bimbo or other. Lady Brayely thinks Cassandra is of the same mould.'

'Mould?'

'Yes, you know, tart. It was when his father was alive and the castle couldn't move for staff. Three months into the marriage he found her pushed up against the wall in the still room with her knickers around her ankles and her skirt around her waist, being given a good seeing to by his father's valet. Apparently it caused all sorts of problems, not least the loss of what was a bloody good valet,' she added, taking a large sip of her drink before picking up her fork and starting on the piece of pie in front of her. 'He divorced her, of course. At least there weren't any children to worry about but, ever since, he's stayed clear of a certain type of woman, until Cassandra that is.'

'I can imagine. And she's got her hooks in, has she?'

'Seems like. Apparently he's arranged to spend the afternoon riding after church, although I'm not sure there'll be any horses involved unless, of course, he gets a better offer.'

'His ankle must be better.'

'What was that? His ankle? It was fine when I spotted him walking across the hall earlier.' She gathered together her plate and mug before wandering over to the dishwasher. 'Oh, I nearly forgot; her ladyship said you might as well have a couple of hours to yourself tomorrow afternoon. She'll only be needing sandwiches for supper. You can borrow me bike, if you like?' she added, rinsing her mug under the tap. 'That's just what the doctor ordered, thanks Tansy. I'll be sure to sleep like a baby as soon as my head hits that pillow.'

She wished she could follow Mary's example but sleep wouldn't come. Usually all she had to do was close her eyes to drift off into oblivion but not tonight. It might have been something to do with her staying up late to start on tomorrow's lunch, a lunch she wanted to be absolutely perfect because chances were it would be her last. It was roast beef.

She'd strolled down to the vegetable patch earlier, the only light coming from the torch they kept by the back door. There was nothing like a nice cauliflower cheese and she had just the right cheese to accompany it tucked away in the back of the fridge. Roast potatoes and light as air Yorkshire puddings all smothered with lashings of her special Dijon mustard gravy. All a bit of a challenge seeing as she wouldn't be returning from church until gone eleven but doable, just.

She'd had a shower and dressed in one of the old t-shirts she kept to wear in bed before weaving her still damp hair into a tight plait. He was right about her hair, she thought peering in the mirror at the golden roots starting to shine through, but there was nothing she could do about them now. Maybe tomorrow she'd find a chemist open, or maybe she'd take to wearing a hat both inside and outside the castle.

Chapter Eleven

'You're up early, Mother?'

'Yes, well, I couldn't sleep.' She turned her head slightly. 'Just toast and a sliver of bacon, Todd,' she said, with a sharp glance at the little pot of baked beans on her son's plate. 'Are you still planning on going out with that person later?'

He laughed, placing his cup carefully back on its saucer. 'That person happens to be a fine horsewoman and I'm just in the mood for a hard ride.'

'Well, she certainly has the bottom for it.'

'Mother, that's beneath you.'

'No, actually it's beneath her – It must be the largest bottom in the whole of Oban,' she added, smoothing marmalade over her toast with a generous hand. 'I do wish you'd settle down with Wilhelmina's daughter. It's my dearest wish, you know.'

'Yes, I do know, mother. But these things can't be rushed...'

'You mean it's still on the cards after that hopeless trip to London?' her eyes on his face.

'Her father is of the same view and, as I don't care one way or the other...' He paused at the lie, because lie it was. It was the biggest lie of all. He wanted her more than he'd possibly wanted anything, ever and if it took marriage then so be it. At least his mother would be happy. He placed his knife and fork neatly in the centre of his plate, his appetite suddenly deserting him. Thirty-four was probably time to think about taking a wife and she'd do. She'd more than do as he remembered the soft texture of her skin under his. He frowned, remembering she disliked him, something he'd have to think about.

He'd also have to think about what game she was playing coming all the way to Scotland. Maybe she'd come to meet him on his own turf or perhaps to get to know him as a man before she accepted, or refused? There would be little likelihood of her being allowed to refuse as he remembered his meeting with her father; a difficult meeting with a difficult man. He'd like to think her father had her best interests at heart. He'd like to think the offer of a dowry was just to sweeten the deal and not the act of desperation by a desperate man. Just why was he so desperate to get her married? Whilst all that stuff in the newspapers was unfortunate it wasn't unheard of for girls like her to be hounded by the press. He could well imagine she wouldn't be able to sneeze without a cameraman handing her a tissue.

She might be pregnant? The thought popped out of nowhere, causing him to clang his spoon against his saucer with a loud enough clatter to earn him a rebuke from his mother. He thought it unlikely but how would he know? If she was, she couldn't be that far gone as he thought back to her flat almost concave stomach. How would he feel if he married her only to find she was expecting another man's child? Would he even know? He scrubbed his hand across his chin, his freshly shaved chin and all he wanted was to be alone for a while.

'You'd make a great dad; just like your father,' she continued, her eyes on her plate and not on the sudden colour infusing his face. 'Best not to leave parenthood too long, you don't want to be chasing them around with a Zimmer Frame.'

Sunday lunch was just like any other Sunday lunch he'd ever eaten at the castle but, now he knew the cook, it was also a surprise. The roast beef was cooked to perfection, slightly pink just the way he liked it. The roast potatoes had the crispiest coating, something that couldn't be rushed and something he couldn't envisage a socialite like Lady Titania Nettlebridge having a clue about. But that's all he knew. She'd even found time to make apple pie with lashings of freshly whipped cream in addition to miniature ginger snaps to accompany their coffee.

He'd seen her, not that she'd have noticed. Oh, she'd have noticed him and his mother being as they were seated in their usual pew right under the pulpit and therefore right under the direct eye of the vicar. He'd watched out the corner of his eye as she'd sneaked in just before the service started. She hadn't been wearing either her black skirt or her jeans. In fact he wasn't quite sure what she was wearing. The eponymous woolly bobble hat had been changed for a plain black beret and then there was a black jacket and something long and slinky underneath. A dress? A skirt? He hadn't a clue, but a deep longing to find out, which wasn't in keeping with his position as both lord of the castle and under the ever watchful eye of the minister. She'd disappeared before the last words of the final hymn had finished their final echo around the nave but he could hardly blame her. He was sure she was avoiding him, or was it him avoiding her…?

'That new cook is a marvel. I wasn't sure when I employed her but that was amazing,'

Lady Brayely said, drawing him back into the conversation. 'Tell her would you, Todd, that the meal was perfectly satisfactory.'

'But you just said it was amazing...?'

'Tor, take a tip from me. It's best not to enthuse too much or else she'll be asking for a pay rise.'

'I don't agree.' He placed his napkin down on the table before pushing his chair back. 'Todd, if you can tell Ti... er, Miss Smith that lunch was amazing.'

Lady Brayely pursed her lips but didn't reply. 'So what time are you meeting Cassandra and, more to the point, what time will you be due back?'

'Now. Whilst I have no plans one way or the other for later I don't expect to be back much before supper. Horses can be unpredictable.'

'So can women,' she mumbled under her breath.

'What did you say?' He paused by the door, one hand on the polished handle.

'Nothing at all. Enjoy yourself, but not too much. Remember, actions have consequences and, if you are betrothed to Titania...'

'Mother, I'm not planning on doing anything foolish...'

'It's not you I'm worried about!'

He wasn't planning on doing anything foolish but he couldn't speak for Cassandra.

He'd joined her at the stables and helped her mount his mother's pretty grey mare, struggling not to laugh at the sight of her ample rear end encased in tight beige riding breeches.

Finally settled she threw him a frown. 'What's up with you then?'

'Oh nothing, I think I just swallowed a fly.'

Leaping into the saddle with ease he was reminded of his mother's comment and smiled. If she wasn't such a haughty piece he'd have told her the breeches were most unflattering; any bigger and he'd recommend she applied for a job on one of those docu-soaps. His eyes travelled upwards, taking in her hacking jacket and pulled back hair. It wasn't that she was unattractive, far from it with her nipped in waist and well-rounded chest. It was just she'd never been his sort with her hoity toity ways and snide remarks. He could never forgive or forget the way she'd treated him as a child. If he'd been a poor man would she even have given him a glance?

'So, where would you like to go then?' he said, trying to make up for the way his mind kept a running comparison between her and Tansy – there was no comparison, or not as far as he was concerned. Would Cassandra be happy to share a fish and chip lunch on Seil and then sleep on an earthenware floor without a complaint leaving her lips? He was a man of simple tastes and simpler expectations. He didn't expect anything from Cassandra and, the way she'd taken the lead without a thought for his wishes, he wasn't going to be disappointed.

'We'll take the long way round and stop off at my parents for afternoon tea.'

He groaned, gently pulling on the reins so that his horse could follow, not that he'd need much prompting. He'd have to be blind not to spot the large target bouncing up and down in front of him. For some reason best known to his brain Tor couldn't keep his eyes away from her bottom and the way it strained against the seams of her trousers. He'd tried a couple of times to take in the view only to find his eyes wandering back in morbid fascination. He didn't fancy her. He didn't even like her and liking had to come first with him; always.

He was suddenly reminded of his first wife. Had he liked her when they'd first met? It was such a long time ago it was difficult to remember with any kind of accuracy, his mind scrolling back over the years. He'd been eighteen and a nervous young man fresh out of school. He'd fancied her rotten the first time he'd seen her, but then most of Cambridge must have felt the same. She was the daughter of the provost and well versed in playing one spotty undergraduate off against the next. He'd fallen hard during that first term and wouldn't have a word said against her. Even Pascal had tried to put him off from offering marriage; they'd fallen out because of it. It was as if he was blinkered to everything apart from her pretty, heart shaped face and lithesome body, a body she knew how to use to its best advantage as his eyes fixed again on Cassandra's bum. If he'd just waited? If he hadn't proposed after about five minutes of dating he'd have realised just what a little scrubber she was but he couldn't see it. It was as if he was blind to every one of her faults. So, no, he hadn't liked her. He'd been infatuated, that was all.

'I wish I had my shotgun. There's that ruddy fox again.' She twisted her head to point at the flash of red hiding under one of the bushes. 'I'll get daddy to come out later to see if he can finish him off. Vermin the lot of them…'

He sighed; hoping against hope the fox would have the sense to disappear into the undergrowth. Cassandra wasn't of the 'shooting above the head' brigade. She wouldn't spare a thought for the fox as a sudden image of Tansy came into his head. Tansy tempting the chickens back into their coop with soft words and caresses. She had them under her spell just as she had him under the same magic potion. There must be something magical to get him, a confirmed bachelor of the been-there-been-divorced-and-not-willing-to-go-there-again variety. He liked her. He liked her a lot. He would just like to know what was going on in that pretty little head of hers. What the hell was she thinking play-acting at being cook; play-acting at being his cook? Oh she was good at it, very good but they were betrothed to be married, for heaven's sake. Her parents were planning for a June wedding with all the trimmings and he certainly wasn't going to object.

He patted Orion briefly on the neck, taking some comfort from the coarse, roan brown mane even as he allowed himself to dwell on that difficult meeting with her father. He'd given permission for their marriage with a ready handshake. He'd pretty much sold her to the first person he could and he was pretty sure it didn't matter what kind of a man he was. He could be a mass murderer or worse but, as long as he had a sizeable fortune and a sizeable title to match, it didn't matter who or what he was as a man. Poor Tansy or Titania as he was trying to think of her. She didn't have a hope with parents like that. She didn't like him, she'd told him as much to his face and yet, married they'd be if his mother and her parents had their way. Married they'd be if he had his way but for a very different range of reasons. The only thing stopping it was if she said no, always a possibility, taking into account her current record. He'd just have to find some way of making that impossible. He couldn't make her like him…

They'd headed across the bridle path skirting the edge of the castle and were making their way down the gentle slope away from the town with distant views of the islands in the background. If he could just avoid looking ahead he'd be fine, more than fine with the rolling hills to the right and the turbulent seas to the left. The road was quiet but three o'clock on a somnolent postprandial Sunday afternoon was never going to be the busiest on Oban's roads. In fact, the only person to be seen in the distance was weaving across the road in the most haphazard of fashions. He couldn't really see, being as Cassandra's bum pretty much obliterated everything in sight but he could hear as the notes of a well-known tune assailed his ears. He smiled openly now at the off-key rendition of 'All about that bass' his eyes lingering for the umpteenth time on that bottom as he heard just how much boys liked booty during the night…

He only stopped smiling at the sound of Cassandra letting off steam yet again. 'Would you just look at that? Look at her taking up the whole road without a care for anyone else,' she said, digging her heels into poor old Daisy's side. 'It's about time someone taught these people some manners...' she added, flying ahead with her whip raised.

He'd never been one for whips or spurs. He'd much rather potter from A to B at a gentle speed. No one used horses as a mode of travel, not for a hundred years or more. Horses were a pleasant break from living life in the fast lane and, if he wanted speed, he'd hop on his motorbike not saddle up his horse.

Now he tapped the side of Orion's flank with a light pat from his open palm as he whispered in his ear. 'Overtake Daisy, there's a good chap,' and within seconds he'd caught up and managed to wrestle both the reins and whip from Cassandra's hand but not before she'd managed to lash out, causing the cyclist to crash into the hedge and then the silence descended.

He'd been holding his breath for the cry, the wail, the scream and nothing. Apart from the slight rustle of leaves and the light patter of hooves scrabbling for footing on the tarmac there was nothing but silence. Silence was the worst sound of all.

Chapter Twelve

Tansy was having a lovely time; a lovely albeit lonely time - not that she'd admit the lonely bit to anyone, especially herself. She'd managed to tidy up after lunch and, racing upstairs, flung off her dress, her only dress, in exchange for her leggings and a thick jumper. Hanging up the black haute couture sheath on its padded hanger she relished for a moment the feel of the silky fabric running through her fingers. She'd packed the dress at the last minute because it could be stuffed in the corner of her rucksack and was just one of those items that looked better without an iron. Her parents were regular churchgoers even if she'd lapsed but she'd just known going to church was something she'd be expected to do in such a small community. In truth, she'd enjoyed sitting tucked away behind a pillar; an observer instead of one of the observed.

Going to church had always been a grand occasion back home, a military procedure ensuring all the boxes were ticked. Hair coiffed. Shoes polished. Matching handbag.

Impeccable nail varnish with none of those chipped bits that were the bane of her life. As often as not, there'd be someone somewhere with a camera or a phone snapping away, trying to catch her out like the time she'd appeared on the front cover of The Sun in odd shoes, something easy to do when she had boxes of the ruddy things in addition to the hangover from hell. Here, life was much simpler as she stared down at her trainers. Here she had a flat pair of black shoes for work, her boots and her trainers. She didn't need any more.

She bundled her increasingly patchwork hair under her hat before hurtling downstairs and out the back door to where Mary had propped her bike earlier. She couldn't remember the last time she'd ridden a bike so it must have been a very long time ago. She must have had a bike but she couldn't really recall, apart from a pink number with the cutest white wicker basket she'd had when she was about six. But riding a bike was one of those things you never forgot or, at least that's what she kept repeating as she wobbled down the drive. Maybe it was the bike's fault? Mary was quite a bit shorter, she mused, looking down at her knees almost bent double. But, whatever the reason, she wouldn't go far, just far enough to escape the confines of the castle and its grounds. She'd never felt claustrophobic before but now… Now she wanted to get as far away from the castle as she could. She wanted to get as far away from him…

If she'd had either the knowledge or the wherewithal to raise the saddle it would have been a different matter but she hadn't so she didn't. Instead, she compensated for lack of stability by increasing her speed. She'd always been a speed merchant be it boats, cars, aeroplanes or motorbikes and she didn't see any need to moderate her behaviour now she was only in charge of a bicycle. She'd had the common sense to check both the tyres and brakes; rudimentary checks nothing like the comprehensive list she ticked her way through each time she took her father's Cessna up for a spin.

She cycled down the hill, coat streaming out behind her, a scream in her throat before easing into what was meant to be a gentle peddle but turned more into a drunken wobble. It wouldn't have been so bad if she'd had a glass of the Rioja Mr. Todd had opened to go with the beef. She was as sober as a judge, soberer if anything being as she hadn't had a drink, an alcoholic drink, since that night he'd rescued her and, with the way she was feeling, there was little point in starting up again. She wasn't a heavy drinker just a social one but if social drinking could culminate in the embarrassment of all embarrassments then she'd quite happily become tea-total.

Starting to hum a tune, a few bars of one of the songs playing on the radio earlier, made her excursion a little less lonely even if it was only the sound of her own voice for company. She didn't know all the words, only a few, but it didn't matter. La La La was perfectly acceptable to anyone that knew anything, anything that is other than the actual words they were meant to be singing. She'd just got to the chorus when she found herself thrown over the handlebars head first into a bush, a holly bush for God's sake.

She lay there, scared to do more than breathe, the sharp edges of the holly leaves digging into her face as she tried to work out what had just happened. She was all alone cycling down the deserted road and then 'Boom'. There had been a sharp pain bite into her cheek… A sting? A branch? She had no idea. Her bicycle, Mary's bicycle had fallen on top of her, pushing her knees into the gravel, her thin leggings being no barrier. She'd have to move but not yet, not just yet.

'What the hell were you thinking, Cassandra? You could have killed her?'

'Not bloody likely and anyway she was scaring the horses with her antics.'

God, it would just have to be them.

She'd have groaned if she wasn't frightened of the spikes wreaking even more devastation.

Tansy wasn't vain more than that. Oh, she was vain in that she liked to make the best of herself and, with a fortune behind her not to mention a pushy mother and a couple of opportunistic friends, she was often portrayed as something she wasn't. She was most comfortable in her jeans, jeans purchased in Knightsbridge but still jeans. She was also careful of her skin. Not for her the hours of beauty treatments being buffed and preened to within an inch of her life. She liked a decent haircut every six weeks and a proper shampoo that wouldn't strip out all the natural oils but that was it. She kept her nails short unless her mother actually dragged her to the nail bar at Harrods but, as far as creams went, she used Ponds, the same cream her grandmother had used until the day she'd died; if it had been good enough for her grandmother, who had the most amazing skin for an octogenarian, it was good enough for her. But, lying there with the feel of pin like needles attacking her face, she was worried. She was terrified because one needle was right under her eye.

There was a gentle hand on her arm, her back and then something shift as presumably the bicycle was lifted.

'Tansy, I need to lift you out of the bush.'

So he recognised her or at least a certain part of her as she felt hysteria build. She'd been runner up in the 'Rear of the Year' competition on more than one occasion so she had nothing to worry about on that score unless her seams had split…

'Please don't…' Her voice caught and stuck in the back of her throat.

'Tansy, it will be alright but I do need to help you…' His hand now turning from a pat to a reassuring massage.

'Tor, you need to shut up and listen,' she finally managed. 'One of the… One of the spikes is just by my eye,' her voice dissolving.

She felt him move. Oh God, she'd made him angry. He wasn't about to leave was he? She wouldn't cope if he just walked away and left. She'd been having such a lovely time and now she wasn't.

Everything was silent for a moment, too silent and then he was kneeling beside her again.

'Tansy, you need to do everything I say, absolutely everything. I'm going to hold back the branches and you're going to ease back gently,' his voice dropping to a whisper. 'Which eye, my sweet?'

'My left, oh do hurry please - I don't think I can put up with this for much longer...'

She heard a rustle above and then in front of her head and suddenly she was free as he shouted.

'Pull back now, Titania, I can't hold them...'

She flopped back onto the ground, tears streaming down her face, red tears as they mingled with the blood but she didn't care. She could open her eyes, both of them. She could see and she certainly could hear as she squeezed them closed again.

She wondered if he'd even realised what he'd said as she felt the heat course up her face. Then she wondered how long he'd known as anger and, it must be said, disappointment grew under her breast in that dark mysterious place where her heart resided. She'd never felt more ashamed or embarrassed as just now.

That photo in the press had angered her. It had disappointed her but she hadn't felt either ashamed or embarrassed. Every time she opened her Instagram tab she came across reality stars exposing a lot more in their airbrushed selfies than she had. It was her parents, or her father to be exact, that had gone off on one. What would the members of his club say? What kind of an example was it setting the servants? For God's sake!

She would have smiled if her cheeks hadn't hurt so much, remembering the big hug Clemmy had dragged her into as she'd contrasted her own muffin top with 'the six pack and fine pair of dumplings' on the front page. 'Worthy of *page three*', she'd added with a wry chuckle.

'Tansy, wake up! We need to get you back home to attend to your face.'

'And your hands, Tor. Don't forget your hands,' Cassandra interrupted. 'You've cut them to ribbons...'

'And just who's fault is that?' he flung over his shoulder as he helped her from lying to sitting and then standing, both arms still round her back as he stared down at her. 'I'm sorry for what she did,' his finger running lightly across the welt on her cheek. 'She had no right to hit you like that.'

Tansy turned and noticed the whip hanging limply from Cassandra's hand but it didn't matter in the scheme of things. So what if she had a ruddy great bruise on her cheek? So what if her face was scarred and disfigured from what felt like a thousand pin pricks? So what? He knew who she was. She'd have to leave. She'd always known she'd have to leave but not like this, never like this. She'd have to leave this beautiful place, a place she'd fallen in love with. No, her eyes now drawn to his hands; his hands covered in blood. She'd have to leave this beautiful place where she'd fallen in love with him, a man who'd never marry her now.

'It doesn't matter. Thank you for helping me,' her eyes avoiding his face. 'I'm sorry you're hurt.' She added, picking up the bike and starting to wheel it back up the hill.

'Here let me help you with…'

'No, I can manage.' her voice sharp. 'Don't you think you've done enough damage,' her gaze now on Cassandra.

Just her luck. The road that before was empty now contained all and sundry out for a stroll. There was the postman, Dick and his wife and then the butcher, Archie, but they didn't stop. One look at her face dripping with what must resemble tears straight from hell and, after a brief "*Hello, what's happened to you, luv*" they ran away as quickly as their little legs would carry them. She must look a fright although, funnily enough, apart from sore knees where skin had embraced tarmac, she felt fine.

She even met Lady Brayely on her way to the rose garden to check on how Jock's new treatment for blackspot was working. It was fortuitous in a way because they both agreed she should leave on the next available train.

It hadn't worked out quite as Lady Brayely had imagined. Oh, her cooking wasn't at fault but she really couldn't employ someone that was obviously so clumsy as to fall into a hedge.

'Just how am I meant to explain it to the neighbours? Did you meet anyone of any importance on the way back to the castle?'

She'd paid her the wages she'd owed in cash, which was a bonus of sorts because how else could she afford to leave? She was pretty sure hitchhiking was out of the question and the £2.60 she had left wouldn't get her past the first bus stop let alone the next train station.

The tears had stopped. Gathering together the household first-aid kit she started cleaning off what she could of the blood, before dabbing on Witch Hazel from the bottle Nanny had insisted she take with her. There was nothing she could do about the weal that went from her eyebrow to her chin but at least the skin wasn't broken as she examined the area with a gentle finger. It was already turning blue and she'd have a ruddy great shiner before the evening was out but it didn't matter. What good were looks anyway when she couldn't have the one man she wanted?

Both Mary and Mr Todd had popped their heads in. She could see they were both upset, but not as upset as she was. She promised to keep in touch but would she? She'd like to think so but it would be too painful. Once her foot crossed back over the threshold of her former life, all she'd want to do was forget the last few weeks.

She was sitting on the end of the bed, if not twiddling her thumbs then passing the time of day staring out of the window. Miss Campbell had popped up with a tray of tea and a bag of sandwiches for the journey but, apart from that, there was silence as the household continued on their day to day activities below stairs. She hadn't heard anything from Tor but then she hadn't expected to. The stables were situated out of the way of the main body of the castle and there'd have been no need for him to come near this part of the house. He might not even be back, her eyes flickering to the watch on her wrist. It was still only 6 pm and, if what Mary said was true, he'd probably still be in bed with Cassandra.

She was bending to pick up her rucksack, her handbag in her other hand when she heard another knock on the door.

'Who is it?'
'Tor. I want to apologise.'
She opened the door only to have it taken from her grasp and closed firmly behind him.
'Hey, you can't come in here. What would your mother or Mr Todd think?'
'My mother; well let's leave her out of it shall we but Mr Todd would be jealous.' She watched him nod his head in affirmation. 'Yes, green-eyed with jealousy,' his eyes lingering on her face with a frown.
'That might have been true earlier,' she started, avoiding his gaze by going to her bedside table and picking up her book. 'And anyway, you have nothing to apologise for. It wasn't you who attacked me.' She gulped back anything else she had to say on the subject of Cassandra and her antics because, of course, he'd support her side of the story over some little cook. Her attention shifted to his hands, his heavily bandaged hands.
'It seems as if I should be thanking you and not the other way round?'
'They're nothing, superficial. I have thick skin,' he added, but there was no smile to accompany his words. Instead he reached up

a hand and tilted her chin so he could examine her face in the light. 'I don't think they'll scar but you should really see a doctor.'

'And what exactly would I say, Tor? That some harpy attacked me with a whip, like something out of a regency novel before shoving me into a holly bush?' She noticed his blush but chose to ignore it, instead shoving on her hat before slinging her bag across her shoulder. 'No, I don't think so, thank you all the same. You really do need to have a word with your girlfriend though. She'll find herself prosecuted if she carries on.'

'You honestly think I'd have a girlfriend when I'm engaged to be married to you?'

'I seem to have missed something somewhere. Oh yes, the proposal.' She raised her hand at the sight of him starting to open his mouth. 'Please don't. The answer is no. It will always be no.'

She eyed him warily. She really had to leave if she wasn't going to miss her train. 'I can't say it's been a pleasure but I have a train to catch if you could...'

'You don't have to go,' he said, running a hand through his hair. 'In fact, I insist you stay. I'll call a doctor. When did you last have a tetanus for instance? What about a course of antibiotics just in case?'

'I'm not a child...'

'Well, don't act like one, Titania. We both know who you are, although I'm still in the dark as to why you'd pretend to be my cook?' he said, continuing to study her with that arrogant look she'd grown to hate. 'It's not as if I haven't been married, I know how a woman's mind works or at least I thought I did.'

'I knew you were married.'

'You knew? Oh, below stairs gossip, I suppose,' his voice suddenly harsh. 'Well, spit it out. What did they have to say? That I wasn't man enough to keep her satisfied? That she had to look elsewhere for her fun and frolics?'

'It wasn't like that.'

'No, you do surprise me.' He heaved a breath, his gaze flickering back to her face, her throat, her chest before continuing. 'So, tell me why you're here - I'd really like to know?'

The colour left her cheeks just as all heat left the argument. She didn't want to argue with him. All she wanted was for him to lift her into his arms and wrap her in the tightest hug but it was too late for that, far too late. Too much had happened for there to ever be a happy-ever-after to this fiasco.

'It was a mistake; a huge mistake and one I regret. I just want to go, Tor. Please let me go,' her eyes huge in death pale cheeks.

'This isn't over. This isn't over by a long shot, Tansy.' He twisted the door knob only to pause before pulling the door towards him. 'I apologise for my behaviour both now and earlier, and that of Cassandra but this isn't the end of it. Go to the doctor for God's sake. I'll be up to see you next week when you're in the mood to discuss things like adults.' His eyes lingered on her as if he wanted to say something, something important but he didn't and the arrogant look, the one she despised more than anything, was back. 'I'll get Toddy to take you to the station,' the door whispering closed on the last of his words.

She sat down on the edge of the bed, reluctant to do anything other than sit. Nanny had been right; when was she ever wrong as she thought back to the last minute Witch Hazel? But a dab of Witch Hazel couldn't solve this problem. This problem was insurmountable. She'd been playing a very dangerous game, a game she'd finally lost. There was no going back to her parents or her previous life. There was no going back to her facile lifestyle of superficial friends and wasted hours. But there'd also be no hanging around waiting for Tor.

She just knew he was going to turn all honourable on her and offer for her hand. But the one thing she couldn't bear was a loveless marriage, a loveless marriage on his side. She had more than enough love for the two of them, but that was useless if he wouldn't accept it. He'd been hurt before by a woman, presumably his wife and now he was unable or unwilling to give his heart to anyone else. Well she couldn't live like that. No, she wouldn't live like that. Her parents could get stuffed. The Press could get stuffed. They could all go to blazes as far as she was concerned as she picked up her belongings and headed for the door. There was only one person running her life and that was Titania Nettlebridge. Tansy Smith was gone forever. She'd start again, she'd have to. But who would she be? What would she do? She'd be true to herself and her own needs for once in her life. She'd bake all day if that's what it took for her to cut the strings to her parents' wallet. She'd make a success of her life not because of but despite them.

Lifting her head she stared at Mr Todd, a sweet smile on her lips as he took her bags.

Being led out of the front door was a surprise but one she couldn't argue with.

'Master Tor insisted, miss,' he said, quietly.

Of course he had. 'Thank you, Mr Todd.'

'The staff will be right sad to see you go, miss. We all loved your cooking,' he added, opening the back door of the Daimler before heading for the boot.

'I'd prefer to sit up front.'

'But the master said…'

'Never mind him; he's not here, is he?' She shut the back door before clambering in beside him. 'The back is so lonely, don't you think?'

'Yes miss.'

'Don't call me that. My name is Tansy.'

Chapter Thirteen

The overnight train from Oban to London
pulled into Euston Station a little after nine.
She was cold, tired and still more than a little
peeved at being dragged out of her seat in the
small hours to change at Glasgow. Whoever
set the timetable must have been having a
laugh or in league with the coffee stand that
was doing a roaring trade in coffee and bacon
butties, a glimmer of an idea sparkling under
her eyelids. The young woman, in charge,
seemed to be managing despite the long
queue. She could do the same. Oh, not bacon
butties as this was London, and not from a
stand but…

'Where to, luv?'

She'd been standing outside Euston Station
in a world of her own. She had a tentative plan
of sorts, a plan that would need a kitchen; a
well-equipped kitchen that would pass all the
inspections. There was only one person with
the right kitchen, but would he help?

She found herself clambering into the back
of the hackney cab because that's what she

did. That's what she always did in London but, with the money from Lady Brayely running through her fingers she'd better learn to take the Tube. She almost laughed at the thought of Lady Titania being photographed clambering aboard the Northern Line along with the rest of the commuters. It would certainly be a refreshing change.

'In your own time, luv. The clock's ticking…?' he said, tapping the black box on the dash with nicotine stained fingers.

'Starbucks then. The one by The Shard.'

'Right you are,' he said, catching her eye briefly in the mirror before swerving into the steady flow of traffic with little regard for the other motorists. She tilted the peak of the baseball cap she'd just purchased before pushing up her sunglasses. It was a disguise of sorts, the best she could do with the limited funds at her disposal. The sunglasses were the largest she could find. The fact they had huge diamante stars at the edges was something she wasn't prepared to think about. They hid her eyes and the upper half of her face and, if she kept her left cheek averted no one would notice the bruising. If she could only stop herself from smiling she'd be able to forget about the incident all together…

'Pssst, over here.'

She'd ensconced herself in Starbucks with a coffee and a newspaper, the peak of her cap pulled even further down her face. She knew she looked like something out of a bad spy movie but, if she didn't want to be recognised for all the wrong reasons, she had little choice. However, when her own brother had just walked past her twice with a barely concealed scowl, she had to resort to other measures.

What he'd say was another thing. Hamilton, her handsome older brother, just oozed professionalism and charm. Bedecked as he was in head to toe Armani, he was the epitome of the successful businessman and she'd noticed at least two other women giving him the once over. Hamilton, who always knew what to say, whom nothing fazed, was fazed now.

'OMG! What the hell?' he said, flipping the brim of her cap with a long finger.

'Shush,' she hissed, throwing a glance over her shoulder. 'Do you want everyone to know it's me?' she added, pushing a cup in front of him before cradling her own large Americano between interlaced fingers. 'I got you a skinny soya latte.'

'Thanks, but I don't understand,' his gaze now focussed on her black ponytail popping out the back of the cap with a shake of his head. 'You drag me out of an investment meeting with the MD for a coffee and a chat? Although I must say the coffee's a whole lot better than the rubbish they were serving.' He leant back in his chair and crossed his legs. 'So what's with the new look then; I hear you've been upsetting ma and pa?'

'That's two questions,' she said, taking off the glasses to show him a glimpse of her black eye. 'I can't very well go around like this, now can I?'

He nearly dropped the cup. Instead he placed it down before taking up her hand. 'Just who the hell did that to you? I'll bloody kill him. No one, I repeat no one messes with my sister.'

'It wasn't his fault.' She paused, gently easing her hand back. 'It was an accident, well part of it was. He tried to help... He wouldn't hurt me, well not physically anyway,' her voice petering out. 'Look, I can't go home like this. If I do they'll just carry on with the marriage arrangements and I can't let them arrange my life for me.'

'They might do a better job than you seem to be doing,' he said, studying her. 'So is that why you've called me then? You want me to what; put you up? Give you a job? Hide you away until you're fit to grace the front cover of Vogue again?'

'Yes, yes, no and partially yes. I've never made it to the front of Vogue.' She smiled, ticking off his questions on her fingers. 'I can sort myself out financially but if you could just put me up for a while, and not tell dad. Oh, and I'll need clothes.' She frowned, thinking about her lack of funds. 'If I get Nanny to put a bag in the garage you could perhaps pick it up on your way home?'

He sighed, his eyes on the legs of an attractive redhead ordering a hot chocolate to go. 'I'll visit them after work,' his gaze finally meeting hers. 'But I won't lie for you. If they ask if I know where you are, I'll tell them.' He stood up. 'I have to go but I expect you to tell me everything that's happened including this man that allegedly didn't beat you up,' his look sceptical as he pulled a key off his ring. 'The alarm code is 5489. For God's sake, don't forget it or write it down, Notting Hill isn't what it used to be.'

Notting Hill might not be what it used to be but it would do fine, more than fine as the taxi dropped her outside the front door of his two-bedroomed, top floor flat in Westbourne Park Road. She often wondered if he'd bought it because he liked it or because of its ideal location. But, whatever the reason, she loved it, not least because he'd stripped out the old, jaded kitchen in favour of an upmarket stainless steel design.

She stopped off at Waitrose on the way and picked up supplies of flour, eggs and butter because the last time she'd visited Hamilton's kitchen all it had contained was a loaf of sliced white, two bottles of champagne and a fridge full of lager. But, with the remains of the afternoon at her disposal, she quickly put on the percolator and set to the first task. She needed to make a list of foods upwardly mobile men and women around London would like to eat; food that could be eaten at the desk, quick bites that wouldn't take long to make but would give her a good return on her investment. Mini bacon rolls were a must after the way the one in Glasgow had revived her for the rest of the journey, but bacon rolls made with designer bread and the best rashers she could afford, topped off with home-made tomato ketchup and Dijon mustard. She'd remembered at the last minute to nip down to the castle kitchen and rescue her jars of yeast and that's where she'd start. Her plan was to create a range of goodies Hamilton could be bribed to take into work. The first would be samples, free samples and with a bit of luck she'd end up getting some orders.

The afternoon flew by and before she knew it, Hamilton's key was turning in the lock. She'd ordered an Indian from the local takeaway at the end of the road and, with a bottle of Chardonnay in the fridge and plates warming in the oven, she was all ready to launch into her new business model. Hamilton's job was working for a bank, taking on new business and what was she if not a new business?

Funnily enough it was her bacon rolls that were the most popular. After that first day when she'd followed Hamilton with trays full of warm, moist bread filled with succulent rashers she had more orders than she knew what to do with. Hamilton's kitchen went from bare bachelor to professional kitchen in less than a day.

Before she knew it, she had three floors on The Shard covered with interest from two others. She was considering looking around for premises in addition to employing a KP at the very least. Whilst Hamilton was the most accommodating, living together would soon start to cause a strain on their usually friendly relationship. It hadn't happened yet but only because she'd ensured she had a home cooked meal for him each evening. There was nothing wrong with takeout food but not every night of the week, as she'd told him on that second evening when he'd come home to beef and ale pie with his favourite cherry trifle for afters. The problems would start when he wanted to bring a girl back…

The issue at the moment was the increasing fraught and frantic phone calls he was getting from their parents. They still had no idea where she was and that's the way she wanted it to remain because, as soon as they found out, they'd be throwing Tor back down her neck; the one thing she couldn't allow.

The days rolled into weeks and before she knew it, she'd been back in London a month and her life, if not back on track was heading that way. She had a job. She had somewhere to lay her head and she had money in her pocket; money she'd earned. She worked. She ate. She slept. That was all. It wasn't enough but it would do.

As soon as she left the apartment, she was looking over her shoulder for anyone that might recognise her. She still hadn't changed her hair colour back from black to blonde and she didn't think she was going to now the roots were starting to grow out at an alarming rate. Funnily enough she quite liked it and, with a dab of hair mascara to blend in the ends, she just said she had a *balayage* if anyone asked.

She continued with the disguises but now, instead of just a woolly or baseball, she had a whole stand of hats in addition to her trusty D&G sunglasses that she wore whenever she left the building. In her new uniform of jeans, boots, hats and sunnies, bearing in mind it was still only April, she certainly got a second look and even the occasional third as she strolled down the street, but never from anyone that recognised her as Lady Titania.

The one person she dreaded meeting, the one person who wouldn't be thwarted by her attempt at disguise was Tor but, after a month, she was getting complacent and even left her hair to fall down her back like the old days not really thinking about where she was or who would see her. Notting Hill wasn't her usual stamping ground and, anyway, word was getting around that Hamilton's sister was play-acting at being a working girl. Only yesterday he'd passed her the phone and she had the first conversation in over a month with her mother. There were tears but not on her side because she had nothing to apologise for. She wasn't the one trying to force her daughter into an arranged marriage. She hadn't stopped her daughter from accessing her bank account. None of it was her fault but, she was left believing it was all her fault; only hers.

The next morning, after an early start, she made her way back to Hamilton's apartment, her basket full of fresh ripe tomatoes for the latest batch of home-made ketchup, only to find it taken out of her hand. Looking up, she expected to find herself staring into the face of a stranger, a stranger desperate to get his hands on her vegetables. Instead she found herself staring at Tor, not that she recognised him.

The man standing clutching her basket was a very different man to the one she'd met in Scotland. In fact, if it hadn't been for his perma-scowl tattooed to his forehead, she doubted she'd have recognised him. No, that wasn't quite true. She'd always recognise him. But - up in Scotland he'd taken little care of his appearance, favouring instead the scruffy student drop-out look over all else. There he'd worn jeans and tatty jumpers and even that day in church he'd opted for a tweed jacket and chinos with an open necked shirt. The one time she'd seen him in a tie he'd been like a tortured soul, moaning under his breath even as she felt her cheeks heat as another memory intervened; the memory of that first kiss.

She examined the bespoke grey three piece suit and white shirt with cuff-links just peeking out from his sleeve with a frown as she allowed herself to take in his paisley tie in muted shades of blue, pink and green. No man had the right to be so bloody perfect. He'd even had his hair cut so now it wasn't too long or too short, just top of the collar length the way she liked it. The question, of course, was what he was doing standing on her doorstep?

'What are you doing here?'

'I could ask you the same thing. I thought you were going back to your parents?'

'I never said I was going back to my parents.'

'No, you didn't, did you? You just let me assume you were.'

She watched him running his hand through his hair, a frustrated look on his face as she hid a smile. She didn't know what he was doing here or what he wanted but she didn't have time for guessing games. She was due to deliver seventy sausage rolls and bacon baps in less than two hours and that meant she had things to do. Picking her keys out of her pocket she let them jangle from her fingers while she stretched her free hand for the basket only to find he'd moved it out of reach.

'Well, I do have to get on. It was good of you to pop by but…'

'You're not going to ask me in for coffee,' he interrupted, 'and after I've come all this way to see you?'

She paused, one foot over the threshold. 'You've come all this way to see me, what did you want to go and do that for? I'm sure I gave you my telephone number and, even if I didn't, you know how to get in touch.' She stared up at him, her mouth open. 'Did I leave something behind?'

'No, you took something with you,' he said, before pushing the door open and gesturing for her to go first. 'I'll carry this upstairs while you make coffee and I'll explain.'

Sitting around the designer metal and glass table in the kitchen was nothing like sitting around the stripped pine one at the castle but she was reminded of it all the same. She was reminded of their early morning tea and even that night she'd thought he was a burglar. She remembered it all; every word, sentence, gesture and smile. She even remembered the frowns as she tried to start up a conversation.

'Have a cake why don't you?' They're a new range and I'd appreciate a second opinion.' She set a plate in front of him with a napkin on the side before lifting the lid of the tin and pushing it towards him.

'New range?' he asked, looking from her to the tin with another beetling of his eyebrows.

'Yes, strawberry and vanilla with chocolate drizzle. It's an alternative to bacon for those that need their afternoon chocolate fix.'

'You've lost me?'

'I've set up a new business,' she said, selecting a cake with care. 'I'm supplying The Shard and other local companies with home baked goodies.'

'You'll make a killing, these are delicious,' he replied, through a mouthful of cake.

'That's what I'm hoping...'

'But why would you be hoping...? Why would you be in need of money with your parents...?' he continued, as he chose another cake from the box with a smile that transformed his face from good looking to heart wrenchingly desirable. She felt herself melt under the weight of his eyes, his stare, his smile. She was just weighing up the pros and cons of leaping across the table when he continued speaking.

'I thought now you were back you'd be slotting into your former life?'

'My former life?' She blinked, shaking off any lingering desire for this inconsiderate git. He'd labelled her a society sweetheart. One of society's leeches who spent all day pampering and preening and all night partying. He might as well have laid the gauntlet in the middle of the table alongside the cake tin. 'That's a joke for a start,' placing her half-eaten cake back on the plate. 'What would you know about my former life? You're a man who spends most of his time looking through a microscope or scrabbling around hillsides collecting samples for... Well, I have no clue what for. You have no idea what it's like being me. You have no idea at all. This is my way of making my mark and I don't care what you think.'

'Whoa. I didn't mean to upset you.'

'I'm not upset.' More like disappointed but instead of getting involved in a conversation that would take them absolutely nowhere, she excused herself before pushing her chair back and heading for the sink. Whilst she'd love more than anything to spend time sitting with him staring at her from the other side of the table there was little point. The tomato sauce wouldn't make itself and neither would the rolls.

'I thought I could take you out for lunch?'

'That would have been lovely but, as you can see, I'm a little busy.' She lifted her head from the pile of garlic she was peeling. 'Lunchtimes have really taken off in the last week and I have tons to do if I'm ever going to meet my orders.'

'What time do you deliver?'

'Twelve, why?'

'If I help, you'll be finished on time and then I can take you out for lunch,' he said, slipping off his jacket and throwing it over the back of the chair before removing his cuff-links and rolling up his sleeves. 'Right, I'm all yours. What would you like to do with me for the next couple of hours?' he added, a playful smile on his lips.

She dragged her gaze away from his strong arms before turning back to the garlic and smashing the cloves with the back of her knife. 'How are you at kneading…?' she asked, after a brief pause.

'Kneading I'm good at. Kneading bread - It can't be that difficult, surely?

She had no intention of accepting his help but not doing something just out of sheer pig-headedness would've been stupid, or that's what she kept telling herself as they assembled piles of mouth-watering savouries. She finally left him for a few minutes while she headed upstairs for a quick shower. He wouldn't tell her where he was planning on taking her but jeans wouldn't hack it. And, anyway, a little part of her wanted to show him just what it was like going out with Lady Titania; he was in for a shock.

Rifling through her wardrobe, she pulled out a plain midnight blue calf-length dress and matching high heels, which would take her from lunch at McDonald's to a meeting with the Queen, not that she expected to be meeting the Queen any time soon. The dress wasn't low cut or high cut, but with its fitted bodice and gently flared skirt accentuated by a thick belt, it whispered sexy and desirable to any man within five hundred yards.

'You look beautiful.'

She glanced at him from under her lashes. She was used to compliments, she was always getting them. And she knew she was a beautiful looking woman but for the first time in a very long time she realised he meant it. She also realised he'd think her beautiful in jeans with ratty hair falling over her shoulders instead of the messy bun she'd opted for. His next comment confirmed it.

'I thought that the very first time I saw you,' as he helped her into the car. 'I thought just how beautiful you were with the kitchen poker in your hand and temper in your heart.' He threw her a look. 'Are you angry with me or just resigned to your fate, Tansy?'

Just how the hell was she meant to answer that? 'I'm resigned to a good lunch but that's all I can commit to at the moment.'

'That's fine by me. All I ask is you keep an open mind,' he added, reaching in the back before presenting her with a bouquet of twelve long stemmed yellow roses.

'We're eating here?' They were in the lift after delivering the trays but, instead of pressing the button for the ground floor, he pressed the button for the 31st and The Aqua Shard. 'They're booked up months in advance. How could you..?'

'I used to go to school with the manager; he pulled a few strings.'

Of course he did. She smoothed her hands over her dress before lifting a hand to tuck a curl behind her ear. She was glad she'd chosen the dress because they sure as hell weren't eating at McDonalds.

'Come on,' he said as the lift pinged. 'He's slotted us in so I don't want to be late. Have you been here before?' he added, grabbing her elbow and directing her towards the bar before ordering a bottle of Chardonnay.

'Only for drinks and it was a very long time ago.'

She'd been here with her parents and her two brothers the evening before she'd moved to Paris. She frowned. She didn't want to think about Paris on a good day. She didn't want to think about Paris any day. Paris was ruined to her. One man's actions had ruined it.

'Are you alright,' his voice concerned as he settled her on a stool. 'I've said something to upset you?'

'No really, I'm fine.'

'No you're not; something about your last time at The Shard?' he questioned softly, his arm shifting from where he had it on his knee to the centre of her back. She could feel the reassuring warmth of his fingers filter through the thin silk of her dress and before she knew it she was telling him.

'Last time I was here was the evening before I went to Paris.'

'Where you learned to cook?'

'Yes, I spent some time with a Michelin chef but it didn't work out.' She picked up her glass and took a large sip. 'I was meant to stay there a year but I came back after a few months...'

'There's something you're not telling me, Tansy,' he said, increasing the pressure on her back slightly. 'Now I wonder what it could be, a love affair gone wrong, perhaps?'

'It wasn't like that. I'm not like that. I was only eighteen for God's sake, straight out of school with no A Levels and...'

'And?'

'And I really don't want to talk about it,' she said, twisting the stem of her glass on the varnished wood. 'Let's talk about something more interesting. So, what brings you to London?'

'Okay, if that's the way you want it,' his eyes boring into hers. 'But you'll have to forgive me if I come up with my own conclusions,' he said, as they followed the waiter to their table. 'I came here to see you. Remember, I did promise. In fact, I was expecting to meet you at your parents a few weeks ago but you weren't there when I visited.' He lifted a hand to tuck the same stray curl behind her ear, his palm lingering on her neck. 'Such beautiful hair, although such an unusual colour; blonde, black and then blonde again, most unusual. I take it you're a natural blonde?'

'What a question, of course I'm a natural blonde.'

'Just like, of course you have 20:20 vision and don't need to wear glasses then?'

She blushed. 'I didn't want you to recognise me.'

'Now I wonder why that was? Not that I'd ever seen you before that day.' He smiled. 'I don't really get much time to read the kind of magazines you appear in, although I am learning. Both Hello and OK have been a revelation, I can tell you.'

She laughed. 'That, I would like to see. I thought people like you only read scientific journals and the like.'

'I do, I did, but needs must.'

'So, you came here to see me?' Her voice soft. 'How did you..?'

'How did I find you, is that what you were going to say?' he interrupted. 'I asked the person I thought who'd know. I asked your nanny.'

'Of course you did, although I didn't tell her where I was staying,' her eyes widening.

'You should know better than that, Tansy. Nannies know everything. She'd put two and two together when your brother, Hamilton is it, came to pick up your clothes. Nice bloke that, we have quite a lot in common.'

'I didn't know you knew him?'

'I didn't. I met up with him last night for a beer.'

So that's where he'd gone, she thought, remembering the way Hamilton had shot off on some pretext straight after dinner with no explanation only to return in the small hours.

'So, what would you like to eat then?' he asked with a smile.

I'm not sure, although I quite fancy the porridge.'

'Porridge? Are you sure you're not looking at the breakfast dishes?'

'No, look.' She tapped the menu with a finger. 'Cornmeal porridge with mushrooms and cheese.'

'I think I'll pass and go for the ribs.' Leaning an elbow on the table he reached across and filled up her wine glass. 'So, tell me, what's next on the agenda for Lady Tansy?'

'Next on the agenda?'

'Yes. Have you moved in with your brother for good or are you going to move back in with your parents? Are you even staying in London?'

'That's a lot of questions, Tor, and I can't answer any of them.' she said, picking up her napkin and unfolding it across her lap. 'For once in my life, I'm making no plans. I'm enjoying setting up my business and…'

'And that all sounds a little lonely. What about dates?'

'What about them? I'm not one of those women that need a man to define them. I'm an independent modern woman who…'

He spread his hands wide. 'Even independent women need love and affection from time to time. I know independent men do.'

She rolled her eyes. 'And you are the man to provide it, are you?'

'We were good together. We are still good together. I asked you earlier to keep an open mind and that's what I'm still asking,' he added, moving his glass slightly to make room for his plate.

Glancing up with a smile, her gaze landed on the table across from them and the two women who were just taking their seats.

'Oh no!'

That's all she needed; her former friends, both of them here and heading her way. She was doomed, more than doomed. There was no way she was prepared to spend any time with them, not after what they'd done. Looking across at the man opposite, even now raising an eyebrow of enquiry at her sudden outburst, she came to a decision. He wanted to be hers; well he could start by getting in a little practice. Leaning forward she raised a hand, tracing her fingers across his face, ignoring his look of astonishment. 'That would be wonderful, Tor, darling. Truly wonderful.'

'Titania. Darling. Whatever are you doing here? We thought you'd fallen off a cliff.'

'Hello Jacinta, Julietta,' she said, standing to air kiss them both. 'I'd like to introduce you to Lord Brayely. Tor, this is Jacinta Fitzarthur-Shloss and Juliette Harrington-Smyde.'

She watched him stand up and hold out his hand. You couldn't fault his manners. In fact, you couldn't fault anything about him from the top of his freshly brushed hair to his impeccable, bespoke tailored suit and highly polished black loafers. He looked exactly what he was; handsome, rich, titled and hers. He wasn't hers but they weren't to know that even as her heart dipped in her chest. He could be hers. Her parents wanted it and she was beginning to suspect, after the yellow roses, he still wanted it. The only sticking point was her.

Her eyes wandered over his broad shoulders and down to his narrow tapering hips. He said they'd be good together but he didn't have to say it. She knew they'd be good together. No. They'd be bloody fantastic and she wasn't just talking about the sex as she felt the warmth of a blush run up her neck. The sex would be amazing but it would lead to the most amazing children, something that was important to her. With their combined looks and his intelligence there'd be nothing to stop them achieving their dreams. There should be nothing to stop her from achieving her dream; her dream of being in Scotland leading a fairy-tale existence. There should be nothing to stop her except the fact he'd never told her he loved her.

He'd joined her now, one hand around her waist nudging their hips together while the other rubbed up and down her arm in the sensual intimacy of lovers.

'So, where've you been then?' Jacinta's eyes fixed on Tor's fingers. 'We tried phoning but..?'

'Oh, really? The reception in Scotland is so bad,' she said. 'Isn't that right, darling?' she added, lifting up her chin and placing a kiss against the corner of his mouth.

'Absolutely frightful, dearest,' the fingers on her waist giving her a gentle nip. 'Yes, well. It was lovely to bump into you both but...'

'We're throwing a little party tomorrow and we'd love you to make it.'

'Oh, I'm not sure. We already have plans.' her eyes seeking out Tor's.

'Sweetie, we were only going out for dinner and I'm sure we can go on afterwards. Now I've met some of your friends, I think it would be a good opportunity to get to know them properly,' he said, tilting his head in their direction. 'I would ask you both to join us for lunch but, as we've nearly finished,' his gaze now on their plates. 'You do have the address, my love?'

Chapter Fourteen

'What the hell were you doing?'

'What?' His voice innocent.

'Agreeing to go to their party? Those two are the reason...'

'The reason for..?'

'The reason I went up to Scotland.'

'The reason you went up to Scotland? I don't understand?'

'Well, understand this. They are not my friends,' her voice cracking. 'I thought they were, but they're not. They were only ever after what they could get, for what they still think they can get.'

He watched as she pushed her chair back before making her way out of the restaurant and, presumably to the restroom. With a wave of his hand he beckoned the waiter for the bill, his gaze still aimed at the door while he waited for her return. He would still have been waiting. She'd have left him waiting forever. After he'd paid and collected her coat and bag he finally caught up with her as she headed across reception to the exit.

'Hey, where are you off to?'

'Lunch is finished. That was all you invited me for, wasn't it, Tor?" she said, ensuring her face was turned away from his.

He knew she was crying. He could see it in the way her shoulders were heaving up and down but he said nothing. He hated wailing women. It was something his female students used to do when things didn't go their own way. His wife used to do it and as for his mother – his father used to call her the *Weeping Willowmina*, something she'd hated above all else.

But Tansy's tears were different as he squashed down the snarky comment building on the tip of his tongue. For a start, she wasn't wailing. Apart from the odd sniffle, there was no sound coming from her at all. She was hiding her distress the best she could and his heart shifted at the thought of her trying to hide anything from him, most of all her feelings.

Was he such a beast that she wasn't prepared to turn to him for comfort? his eyes drawn to her averted head. He realised, with a start, he'd been alone so long he'd forgotten what it was like to be with a woman in more than the work setting. He knew he was short tempered on occasion but for her to turn away from him the way she was doing was a salutary lesson. She'd cried the last time too, he remembered. She'd cried when she'd been hurt and in pain but these tears were different. It was as if something was breaking inside, something he couldn't heal with a hug or a smile. He wanted to draw her into his arms, resting her head on his chest as he rubbed her back; as he absorbed her sadness onto his own shoulders but she wouldn't want that.

Instead of doing what he wanted, for once, he did what he felt she'd accept, at least from him. Draping her coat over her shoulders he took hold of her elbow with a gentle hand and directed her towards his car.

'I don't need a…'

'A lift? Where I come from, the date doesn't end at the restaurant door. I'll see you home first.'

'What are you doing here?'

'Well, that's a fine welcome, I must say. Here I am with supper and all you can say is *what are you doing here.*'

The afternoon had passed on wings and now he was back at her door for the second time that day, for the second attempt in the art of seduction, or should that be courting? He didn't want to seduce Tansy. No, that wasn't quite true. He did want to seduce her but only after the wedding ring was securely on her finger with extra-strong Superglue. He'd waited this long, he could wait just a little longer. So, here he was for *act two*. He had food, he had beer, he had chocolate…

'Hello, Tor. Now what are you doing here?' she added, her eyes on the bag as she placed both hands on her hips. 'And more importantly what's for supper? Hamilton is out tonight so I…' She threw him a look laden with suspicion. 'Funny that, Hamilton being out? He's only just texted about a last minute business meeting. You wouldn't have anything to do with that, would you?'

'Me? If I was meeting Hamilton for a business meeting what would I be doing standing at your door?'

He watched her sigh in frustration.

'You'd better come in then, although I hope it's not Chinese. I'm allergic.'

'No, I knew that. That's why I got Indian,' he replied, following her into the kitchen.

'How did you know, I don't remember ever telling you?'

'Oh, I'm sure you must have said, otherwise how would I have known?'

'I have no idea.'

She took out a couple of matching plain white plates in addition to forks and a serving spoon while he removed boxes and cardboard covers to reveal chicken tikka masala and rice with fluffy naan bread.

'Now, I really am suspicious,' she said as she joined him. 'How did you know chicken tikka is my all-time favourite?'

'Oh, lucky guess, I suppose,' he said with a twinkle before starting to serve her.

'A likely story. I forgot drinks, what would you like? We have…'

'All sorted, Tansy,' he said, pulling out a couple of bottles of Cobra before using the bottle opener on his keyring to flip off the tops. 'You can't have curry without Indian beer, it's a rule.'

She laughed. 'And just who's rule would that be?'

'Not mine,' he said, joining her in a wry smile. 'Anyone who's shared halls of residence would tell you.'

'Ah, well that's where we differ then. I'm thick; I never made it to university.'

He took her hand and, turning it over gently encased it between his own. 'We can't all be the same. You have skills, special skills that I couldn't dream of having.'

'Like what? Making bread is easy,' she said, tearing off a piece of naan and handing it to him.

'Not the way you make it. We all agreed at the castle that none of us had ever tasted anything like it.' He smiled, looking her in the eye. 'Why do you think you've suddenly hit it at

The Shard? It's certainly not from lack of competitors. Hamilton was telling me as soon as they tasted your bacon rolls they sacked their previous supplier.'

'He didn't tell me that. If I'd known someone else was supplying them...' She frowned.

'I wouldn't worry about it. I'm sure they have enough business to be going on with, and anyway I've had those sorts of sandwiches before and they're not a patch on what you make.'

'I didn't think mycologists would be attending meetings at The Shard?'

'Yeah, that's what you know,' he said, leaning forward and tapping the end of her nose with his knuckle. 'I also have a castle and lands to run and sadly, money doesn't grow on trees. Someone has to pay for it all. Someone has to ensure the tenant farmers are well looked after. For that I need money. And for that money to work, it needs to be invested, hence my occasional meetings at The Shard. Although I have to say, I do keep them to the minimum,' he added, glancing down at his jeans and pristine white shirt with the cuffs rolled back. 'As you can probably tell, wearing a suit isn't my thing. In fact this is well-dressed for me.' His eyes now on her leggings and scruffy T-shirt with the words *bread is the meaning of life* emblazoned on the back and the picture of a *baguette* on the front. 'I like the T-shirt by the way, very fetching!' His gaze now on her chest and where it moulded to her frame with all the precision of a second skin.

'You would,' as she quirked an eyebrow. 'It shrank in the wash and, as I wasn't expecting visitors, I didn't think anyone would see,' she said, taking a sip from her beer.

'Really, I thought you'd be out on the tiles with your friends?'

'Those two are no friends of mine and I have no idea why you accepted the invitation. I've a good mind not to go.'

'Oh, you are going and I'm going to escort you. Did you never learn that attack is the best form of defence or that revenge is a dish best served cold? I don't know what it was they did to upset you but, surely that's over? I'll be around to keep you out of their *dastardly clutches*,' his voice now a cross between a Dalek and Darth Vader as his hands clawed towards her neck.

She eyed him over the top of her beer. 'You don't understand what you're doing messing with those freeloaders. It's only taken me the last fifteen years to realise the less I see or hear of them, the better. I'll go to the party but that's it. Please don't accept any more invitations from them because I certainly won't be attending and no more of the funny voices already. You're not that good.'

'I'm wounded to the core.' His hand clutched to his chest.

'Well, be wounded and while you're doing the dying duck act, what about a coffee before you go?' she said, starting to gather together the empty plates.

He glanced at his watch with a smile. 'It's a good job I brought along pudding then isn't it or you'd be throwing me out before the clock has even reached eight? Is that pumpkin time, sweetheart?' he added, reaching into the bottom of the bag and producing a box of triple chocolate muffins. 'Obviously they won't be as good as yours but…'

'As long as I didn't have to make them, they'll be fantastic,' she said, grinding coffee beans before adding them to the top of the peculator. 'Whilst I love cooking, its lovely to eat something you haven't cooked for a change, which makes the Indian and then pudding all the more enjoyable, so thank you. I'm sorry I'm a bit of a wet blanket at the moment but those two always get me down and…' She threw him a sweet smile that had his heart leaping about in his chest like a kangaroo on a trampoline. 'And you're not that bad at accents. You're not that good but better than I made out.'

He raised his beer bottle to her.

'Here's looking at you, kid.'

Sitting beside her on Hamilton's sofa in front of the wood burner with a mug cradled on his lap was one of the most enjoyable experiences. She'd lowered the lights and, fiddling with one of the remotes on the coffee table, had put on some soft playing music in the background. He didn't know what it was but the gentle notes punctuating the air with melody made the evening perfect. Or at least it would have been perfect if she hadn't been hugging the other end of the sofa as if her life depended on it. He smiled to himself at the sight of her with her feet tucked under her, her head resting back as she listened to the music. This was contentment. This was happiness. This was pure unadulterated love, just this – here – now – with her.

He never wanted it to end but, with the clock ticking towards eleven, it was time to go. He'd promised Hamilton he'd leave before midnight, a grin appearing. Hamilton had offered to spend the evening at his parents but not the night. He'd need to know quite a bit more about him if he was going to allow him stay the night with his sister. Good he didn't know about Belnahua then or he probably wouldn't have agreed to make himself scarce. If he'd had a sister he'd have liked a brother like Hamilton to be there for her. He was a good man, or he would be if he could only get him on his side.

Stretching his arms above his head he went to stand.

'Well, thank you for a lovely evening but I suppose it's time I was going.'

She glanced up in surprise. 'Where are you spending the night?'

'Why, are you offering to put me up?'

He noticed the blush score her cheek with amusement even as she said a resounding no. 'Hamilton only has two bedrooms and I'm sure he wouldn't give up his bed for you.'

'And your bed wouldn't be big enough to share?'

'I'm not offering you my bed, Tor. I'm not offering you anything even a...' She didn't finish the sentence, her eyes wide. 'You're not heading back to Scotland this late are you?'

'No, you seem to have forgotten that tomorrow I'm escorting you to the party you don't want to go to. But, to make it up to you, I'll take you out for dinner first.'

'There's no need to do that...'

'Yes, there is; every need. Put your glad-rags on because, if there's time, we might go dancing. That is, if you'd like to?' he added.

She joined him at the door and placed a hand on his arm. 'I'd like to know why you're doing this?'

Settling her arm around his waist he cradled her face within his hands, smoothing the pad of his thumb across her cheek. 'It's time we got to know each other. I like you, I like you a lot. In fact,' he paused, his eyes flickering away before returning to her face. 'In fact, I'd like to marry you,' his head dipping towards her.

She tasted of coffee and chocolate, her lips silken sweet under his, and if he died now he'd die a happy man. A lightning bolt could cleave out of the sky and pin him to the ground and he wouldn't care a jot. The only thing he'd care about was leaving her behind. Holding her within his arms was the happiest he'd ever felt. What he'd had with his first wife couldn't have been love because it hadn't been anything like this. Now he was with somebody who meant more to him than life itself, although she obviously didn't feel quite the same as he felt her starting to pull away.

'So you're what, you're wooing me?'

'If that's what you'd like to call a proposal of marriage, then yes,' his mouth pulled into a thin line. 'So I take it your answer is no?'

She placed a hand in the middle of his chest, reaching behind him to open the door.

But before she pushed him out she raised her lips to his for the briefest whisper of a kiss.

'Yes, that's a no; a no for now. But carry on with the wooing, I quite like it.'

Chapter Fifteen

She missed him the following day and she didn't like it, she didn't like it one little bit. She knew he'd said he'd see her in the evening but that didn't stop her looking over her shoulder every five minutes; that didn't stop her glancing at the phone and that didn't stop her thinking about him every second of every minute of every hour.

After she'd delivered the lunchtime order to The Shard, she nipped into a taxi and headed for Harrods. Taking the escalator up to the 'woman's floor' she shook her head in disgust. She had more than enough clothes and shoes but tonight she wanted to wear something special, something extra-special. Tonight she wanted to wear something that would blow his socks off. She giggled at such a stupid phrase and wondered who had come up with it and then she forgot all about socks.

'Lady Titania, how wonderful to see you again. You haven't brought your mother with you today?' she added, looking over Tansy's shoulder.

'Er no, just me.' She smiled at the wiry shop assistant. Her mother was a big spender on the woman's floor and, of course, these shop assistants would be on commission.

'And you've changed your hair. It's, er, so unusual,' she added.

'Yes, well I fancied a change,' she said with a little shrug. 'I'm in need of a new evening dress, something long and slinky but with just enough movement for dancing,' her eyes drawn to the rails upon rails of designer dresses.

'I have just the thing and it only came in today so nobody else will be wearing it. Still a size 8, I see. If you'd just like to go to the changing room, I'll get my assistant to bring it through for you.'

The dress was divine, more than divine. Jenny Packham had always been a favourite but she'd surpassed herself with layers of creamy, tulle swathing a plunging halter-neck with the cutest cinched velvet waistband and jewel encrusted detailing around the neck. It was long, romantic and, when she slipped it over her head, she felt utterly gorgeous. All she needed was a prince but as she already had a castle on the table, she'd happily make do with a viscount. It wouldn't be such a great hardship, her face a study in merriment as she swished the skirt around her ankles.

The only thing she wasn't sure about was the colour. Ivory had such a bridal virginal air about it but it was the only colour they had in stock so it was that or carry on searching and the clock was ticking. However, she did balk at adding shoes to the shopping bill despite the asserted attempts of the shop assistant. She had enough in her bank account to pay for the dress, but not shoes. There was always her mother's account but there was a big difference between a couple of skirts and shirts for work and a bit of frivolous nonsense meant for fun, her hand lovingly pleating the fabric between gentle fingers.

She had the dress.
She knew where the shoes where (bottom rack, fifteenth box from the left).
Her hair was a completely different animal…

Her hair was the only thing worrying her because she'd heard horror stories of black hair being dyed blonde and turning green or, God forbid, orange. Whilst she liked both colours she didn't really think her parents would consider a traffic light look appropriate for their only daughter.

The hair stylist was more than helpful and immediately shifted her calendar to make room. It was wrong, Tansy knew it was wrong, but in the same way Tor had managed to secure a table at The Shard, she accepted it as part and parcel of been titled *and* she would leave a hefty tip. After flicking through magazines, they decided on trimming her hair from waist length to just below her shoulders and adding subtle blonde highlights to the ends to try and blend the blonde roots with the starkness of the black. She advised her against dying it blonde so she'd just have to live with the choc-ice look for the time being.

Tor was speechless when she opened the door, her cashmere throw draped over her shoulder as she shouted 'goodbye' through the kitchen to Hamilton.

He was leaning against the jamb with a bouquet of the sweetest bunch of peonies in shades of cream and pink. He'd stopped off at the first florist he'd come across and taken ages choosing just the right flowers for just the right woman. There were roses in abundance, in all the colours but he'd given her roses already. Orchids were too manufactured, too stylised, but peonies; peonies with their glorious full-bodied blooms almost too large for their slim necks were perfect.

She looked just like she would on her wedding day, their wedding day, because he wasn't giving up yet. He'd never give up, even if he died trying. The dress skimmed her curves before draping her hips and flowing to the floor where his heart joined it. He could hardly think, he could hardly see. He was fit to burst with love, with desire, with longing. Before he knew it he was doing what he'd promised he wouldn't. He reached in for a tender kiss before dropping on to one knee.

'I was going to wait until later but Tansy, will you marry me?' he whispered, removing a small Chopard ring box from his pocket.

She stared at the box, her face blanched pale before placing her hand over his and pushing it back towards him.

'Ask me after the party.'

Dinner was at *La Cage Imaginaire*, along Flask Walk and within walking distance of Julietta's Hampstead apartment. They both chose Scottish fillet of beef, laughing when they realised it was on the menu. Sitting at the white damask covered table with sparkling cutlery and glassware they could have stayed there all evening, hands entwined as they talked and talked about their childhood growing up in very different and yet surprisingly similar circumstances. They both had ponies as children and then horses, spending most of their spare time in the stables. Where Tor had gone to university, Tansy had left for Paris but she skipped over that part. They both loved to read, although their tastes weren't similar. They even enjoyed the same movies although Tor raised his eyebrows at Notting Hill being her favourite.

'It was always going to be popular but with Hamilton living almost opposite William Thacker's blue door...'

'William Thacker?' His look blank.

'You know? Oh dear, you don't, do you? Well, at least I didn't say The Sound of Music,' she added with a giggle.

'There is nothing wrong with The Sound of Music. I'll have you know I was brought up on Julie Andrews and Mary Poppins.'

'Really, well you are a little older than me.'

'I'll give you older. They were on DVD,' he said, leaning across the table and stamping a kiss on her lips.

'What's that for?'

'For being cheeky.'

'I'll have to be cheeky more often,' she said, placing a finger to her lips with a smile. 'So, you never did tell me what you were doing on Belnahua?'

'You're sure you really want to know? It's not very romantic.'

'Let me be the judge of that, I think it's the most romantic of places.'

He grinned, remembering their first night together, hopefully the first of many. 'I'm working with some boffin friends of mine in Cambridge on research into the origins of man.' He paused, his eyes seeking hers and the boredom he was sure to find.

'Go on then. So, you're a modern day Charles Darwin?'

He laughed. 'Not quite. Darwin got to travel to South America while the islands of interest are on my doorstep so to speak. Anyway, last year these chaps found a fungus on the island of Kerrera that turned out to be four hundred and forty million years old. It certainly ruffled some feathers, in the world of mycology I can tell you. Since then I've been helping them to collect and analyse fossilised rock and soil samples from all the other islands in the Inner Hebrides, all 79 of them.' He looked up suddenly. 'Bored yet?'

'Never bored. So what's this fungus called then?'

'Tortotubus, a conversation stopper if ever there was one. What would you like for dessert?'

They walked, or should that be shuffled, to Julietta's a ground floor apartment along Pilgrims Lane. Tansy had opted for her four-inch Manolo Blahnik crystal brooch embellished Hangisi pumps, which she hadn't actually bought to walk in.

'Slow down, why don't you? You try walking in these,' she said, lifting her skirt and trying to run after him with little baby steps.

He paused to stare, his eyes twinkling with laughter.

'How did you ever know? I've lost count the amount of times I've worn ladies clothing and as for footwear… Although I do have to get my size nines off the Internet. I have a nice pair of Jimmy Choo's in green if you'd ever like to borrow them,' he added with a grin. 'I'm happy to carry you but I wouldn't like to crush your dress,' as he swung his arm over her shoulder and slowed his pace.

'I'll hold you to that. The only way I'm going to be able to get through it is by getting drunk, so watch out.'

He swung her to a pause under a convenient lamppost, which illuminated her face to a translucent beauty. 'In that case, I might as well get my money's worth while you're still standing,' he said, his lips meeting hers. His body moulded to her, his hands intertwined with her; his heart matching hers beat for beat.

They could've stayed like that for minutes, hours, days, forever and when, they finally broke apart, they still touched.

'Do we really have to go to the party?' he asked.

'Well, it was your idea in the first place.'

'I know, but I've changed my mind.'

'No, I need to be brave; I need to meet them one last time and then walk away,' her hand reaching up and caressing his face.

'After...' His look uncertain, his speech stumbling. 'I'm staying at Browns Hotel if you'd like to come up for a nightcap?'

'What, to see your etchings? She laughed her reply before pressing a kiss against his lips. 'Yes, my darling, I'll come up and see your etchings and, if you still want to ask me that question?' She pulled on his hand. 'Come on, the sooner we get this thing over with, the sooner we can go dancing.'

Julietta opened the door after one knock as if she'd been standing on the other side waiting for them.

'Come in, Titania, lovely to see you and your little friend,' she said, dragging her into a briefer than brief hug with another one of those non-touch air kisses she was famed for. Tansy gave her a small smile as she took in her sprayed on black body stocking and bright red high-heels, no doubt colour coordinated to match her bright red lipstick.

Julietta was someone she'd thought a friend, a best friend even. She was someone she'd shared her secrets with, all of them. No one knew her better than Julietta and yet she suddenly realised she didn't know this woman in front of her. This woman was a stranger, a complete stranger and someone she didn't like very much. The way she grabbed on to Tor's arm, her blood dipped fingernails clutching at his jacket as if she was staking a claim; perhaps she was? Perhaps she'd been too hasty in agreeing to go back with him after the party. He had proposed but being engaged wasn't what it used to be, not that she was engaged. She was nearly engaged – there was a wealth of difference between a yes and a maybe.

'You know some of the people here already,' Julietta added, gesturing with her hand towards the lounge. 'What would you like to drink?'

She didn't want anything to drink. She didn't want anything to eat as she saw one of the guests wandering past with a slice of floppy quiche. All she wanted was to release Tor from this bitch's clutches and run for her life. She was up to something, the question was; what? No doubt she'd been paid handsomely by the gutter press for that photo opportunity tip-off. No doubt she'd spent all the money by now…

She shook her head trying to puzzle it out, even as she watched Julietta run her gaze from the top of Tor's head to the soles of his shoes as if he was some prize exhibit. She couldn't blame her, not really. He looked good enough to eat, dressed as he was in another one of his suits. For a man who professed not to like them, he certainly seemed to have a wardrobe full. This one was black with a satin collar, the snug fit only emphasising his strong build. He'd left his tie at home, instead leaving the top couple of buttons open to reveal a thick column of deep brown throat, a throat she was having difficulty in dragging her eyes away from.

She still hadn't answered. She didn't want to be rude in case she was wrong. She couldn't think outside of the fact she didn't want to be here.

'A wine for Tansy and I'll have a beer if you have it?' Tor answered, throwing her a worried look.

'Beer? I'm not sure what we've got.' She paused, flicking her blonde fringe with a smile. 'Why don't you come and help me, Lord Brayely while Titania circulates?'

She wandered into the lounge simply because she didn't have a choice. Tor had been manoeuvred out the way, which scuppered her plans for heading out the front door. As soon as the coast was clear, she'd drag him away and, if he didn't want to be dragged she'd leave without him. She was experienced at running away, this would be a doddle after Paris, London and then Scotland.

The lounge wasn't as crowded as she'd expected. In fact, it was nearly empty. There were a cluster of friends standing by the fireplace and one or two sitting on the stark white leather sofas but that was it. She glanced around at the plain white walls punctuated with designer arty paintings depicting large oranges and pears. She wasn't a snob, far from it but she really didn't get Julietta's taste in art. The room looked like a dentist's waiting room with its laminated wood flooring and designer coffee table with a couple of carefully positioned books on the centre.

She didn't belong here. She'd never belonged here as she looked around at the women crawling with diamonds and jewels. What had they done with their day that was of any use? It was a dead cert it involved the full treatment of waxing and polishing with perhaps a spray paint for all those nooks and crannies that needed it, her eyes now on her own short unvarnished fingernails. Some of them had obviously gone one step further in the strive for self-improvement by having their tyres pumped, her eyes drawn to Jemima's stunning low cut dress and her fine display of mountains where before there'd been barely a couple of minor speed bumps. She smiled to herself at the analogy remembering her very busy afternoon. After the hairdresser, she'd visited her parents; a difficult half hour spent over cucumber sandwiches saying very little but giving her the opportunity to reclaim her laptop.

Instead of facials and spa treatments, she'd spent the rest of the afternoon on her book, the book she'd been meaning to write for years but never had the nerve. When everyone tells you you're thick, you start believing it. She couldn't spell and as for punctuation; the semicolon was a puzzle, as was the apostrophe but it was the use of ellipses that she found the most confusing…

Sitting at the kitchen table, she decided to ignore the finer elements of grammar and just get her words down and, before she knew it, she was already halfway through the introduction. The words had flown from the ends of her fingers but then again, she was talking about something she understood. She was talking about a passion, her passion. She was talking about bread. She'd only powered off when she heard Hamilton's key in the door and then it was a mad dash to get ready for the party she didn't want to go to.

She crossed the room to the pine mantelpiece with its measly gas fire and joined in a dulcet conversation with a couple of girls she'd been at school with. She didn't know them well but she could get away with giggling over Latin lessons and the science teacher's comb-over. After a while she got bored. Tor had obviously been hijacked and all she wanted to do was leave. The music was loud and obnoxious and the wine mediocre. She would've gone searching for him but she wouldn't give Julietta the satisfaction. Instead, she found herself heading towards the patio doors and the bench at the end of the garden screened off from the road by a wall of pampas grass. It was dark and quiet with only the stars to keep her company. Closing her eyes she avoided thinking about Tor and what he was up to. Instead she let her mind focus on her book and chapter one.

'*Bonsoir* Tansy.'

Chapter Sixteen

'So how long have you known Titania then?'
'A little while, I'm friends with her brother.'
'Which one?'
'Hamilton.'
'Ah, my favourite. I'm so pleased she's staying with him,'

He missed her sharp look as he took a sip of his drink. If he had, he wouldn't have allowed himself to incline his head, but he was too busy with his thoughts. He didn't want to be here holed up next to the fridge with this woman. Her eyes were too close together for a start; too close together and too small and beady. Was beady even a word? Whatever, it suited her. Tansy was right. The only question he had was, what had she ever seen in her?

He regretted making her come to the party. They could have been dancing by now. He could have been twirling her around, her sensual skirt flowing over those wonderful legs. Not that he'd ever seen her legs, he reminded himself with a start. He'd seen the outline of them under her leggings and he'd seen her ankles earlier as he'd helped her down the steps but that was all. He'd also seen her feet, as he remembered that evening with Toddy, but he would like to see a little more of her than her ankles and her feet. There was her bottom of course, that wonderful curve he knew like the back of his hand as the sudden image of her sticking out of that hedge appeared in his head. She had a good bum. No, she had a fantastic bum and he was pretty sure her legs would be of the same mould.

He withheld a laugh at the correlation between his love of all things mouldy and his love of all things Tansy. They were his two passions but he'd give up the first in a heartbeat. She'd crawled under his ribs up to his heart and, just like her namesake, she'd invaded him more effectively than any military campaign. It was a war he had no intention of winning. It was a war he had no intention of competing in. It was a war and he was surrendering.

He felt the increased pressure of Julietta's hip as she pressed up next to him. This was no friend of Tansy's the way her hand, so recently on his arm, was creeping towards his back. He knew what she wanted. No, that wasn't quite true, he added with a frown. He knew if he gave her even a hint of encouragement, she'd whisk him upstairs but she wouldn't lock the door. She'd want to be found. She'd want Tansy to find them. The colour drained from his face. If she walked in now she'd reach all the wrong conclusions.

'Hamilton was always such a darling, the clever one of the family. Poor Tansy hasn't got two brain cells to rub together.'

'Brains aren't everything and Tansy is very talented in her own way. We can't all be rocket scientists, can we? What do you do, Julietta?'

'Me? As little as possible!' She laughed. 'Daddy left me a small trust fund and along with a few hours spent at an art gallery along Bond Street, I scrape by. What I'm looking for is a sugar daddy or even a toy boy to keep me in the manner I'd like to become accustomed...' she added, reaching up to brush his hair off his forehead.

Grabbing her wrist, he forced it away from him and dropped it like a hot potato. 'Well, good luck with that, I think I'll go and see where my date is.'

'Oh, she's probably in the garden with lover-boy. You have met her lover, haven't you? He's French,' a malicious gleam in her eye.

Tansy was right, as he put his bottle down on the littered table and headed out the door, the echo of her laughter resounding in his ears. This woman was evil personified and he was the one who'd put her back in her clutches.

He walked into the lounge but there was no sign of her. Making his way through the patio doors he headed into the garden and there she was, just as Julietta had predicted; in a deep clinch with someone. No, not someone. Some man. A stranger.

All he could do was watch. It was as if he'd been frozen just like the life-sized statue of David in the corner. But this was no Goliath up ahead. This wasn't a battle he could win with the throw of a stone, his eyes fixed on that one spot he couldn't bear to look at and yet couldn't turn away from. This 'Goliath' of a man was all over her, his hands in her hair, on her back, on her hips, roaming up her skirt, lips pressed against the side of her neck as he muttered words only intended for a lover's ears.

He knew it was wrong but he started translating with his school boy French all the same. If he'd been German, or Dutch for that matter, he'd have had no chance but French he could do. Of course, this man was going to be French. He was the Frenchman she'd refused to talk about. He was the Frenchman she'd refused to talk about, saying the words he wanted to say to her; words he should have said to her. He'd repeated them often enough in his head so why not out loud? He'd shied away from saying them in case she hadn't felt the same and now… and now it was too late, far too late.

Je t'aime de tout mon coeur. I love you with all my heart.
Fais-moi l'amour. J'ai besoin de toi. Make love to me, I need you.

He felt like a voyeur. No. He was a voyeur. This was her personal privacy he was invading like someone after a cheap thrill. He couldn't be here any longer. He couldn't bear the agony of his heart dissolving into a haze of unfilled hopes and dreams.

Turning on his heel he started walking back up the garden that is until he saw a movement out of the corner of his eye and then a camera flash but not just one camera flash, it was like a thousand bulbs going off in his head and then she was running. She was running towards him, tripping, taking his hand, grabbing and pulling him back into the house, out the front door, down the path and into the street before turning down a narrow unlit lane separating one row of back gardens from the other. Kicking her shoes into the gutter she continued running, tears streaming down her face and all he could do was pick up her shoes and chase after her.

'Hey stop, your shoes,' he dragged her to a halt, his hands on her shoulders but she pulled away; her eyes frantic. Her gaze looking everywhere except at him.

'I'm not Cinder bloody Ella, Tor. I don't care about the shoes. In fact I never want to see them again,' she added, taking them out of his hand and stuffing them into one of the dustbins lined up ready for collection.

'I don't understand…'

'Don't you? Don't you, Tor? You have no idea what's just happened?' She moved her hands to her legs as she bent forward and tried to catch her breath. 'Funny, I understand it all but then it's happened to me before. You've never been splattered across the front pages like I have.'

'That man you were with. The Frenchman. Your boyfriend, I take it?'

'No,' she heaved a sigh. 'That wasn't my boyfriend. But it doesn't matter now, does it?' She lifted up her skirt, treading carefully over the cobbles. 'The damage is done. You'll read about him tomorrow, but all I ask is don't believe everything you read because none of it will be true. We never… I never…' She caught his eye and, stretching out a hand went to touch his face only to pull back at the last minute. 'Tor, I just want to go home.'

'But what about?'

'Please,' her eyes imploring, beseeching and finally begging him to stop questioning her. 'I can't deal with this now. Tomorrow, I'll call you tomorrow.'

But tomorrow was too late.

Chapter Seventeen

'OMG, you've really blown it now,' her brother said, walking into her bedroom and throwing a pile of newspapers down on top of the duvet.

'What are you talking about, Hamilton? All I need is a couple of paracetamol for this headache, and to have you wittering on about something I already know about is unbearable,' she said, her hand on her brow.

'Something you know about? Are you sure about that, really sure? So you know all about being cited as co-respondent in a divorce then,' he mumbled, turning towards the door.

'What!'

'That's right. That poncy French chef, whatever his name is. There are photos all over the newspapers of him with his hand up your skirt and his tongue down your throat. His wife's lawyers are having a field day. It's just the ammo they needed for her to divorce him and, if the article in The Mail is right, you'll be receiving an official letter in the post any day soon. Well done, sis, very well done. You had

Tor dangling from the end of your rod and you let him go. I don't know what the parents are going to say. It's unlikely they'll be able to magic up another suitor for your hand, not after this fiasco.' He paused at the door. 'I'll drop you up some paracetamol and some tea and then I need to think about a way of running the gauntlet.'

'Running the gauntlet,' her voice a thread of sound.

'Yes, we have the whole of the British press camped outside my door thanks to you. Apparently, according to The Sun, it's *Notting Hill* all over again. They're just waiting for me to do a Spike on the doorstep in my Y-fronts and then their day will be perfect.'

'Oh.'

'Oh indeed. The only thing I can say is it's a good job I don't wear them.'

'You don't wear underpants?' Her eyes wide. 'You mean you go commando?'

'No. I'm a banker.' He rolled his eyes. 'I mean, I wear boxers.'

'At least that's something,' she muttered, brushing the papers away before hopping out of bed. 'There's nothing I can say as an apology but I can get you out of the house without anybody seeing you.'

'How can you?' He raised his eyebrows. 'We're surrounded.'

'No we're not. They won't think about the back gate, it's well hidden behind next door's laurel hedge. I'll get the Kowalczyk's from the garden flat to let you out.'

'How do you know the names of the people on the ground floor?'

'I've met them a couple of times although I don't know him but his wife is lovely. She makes a mean rye bread…' She reached up and dragged him into a deep hug. 'I'm sorry for causing any embarrassment. I'll head back home later and face them.' She paused. 'If Tor gets in touch, although I can't believe he will for a minute, just tell him I don't want to see him. Not now.'

Chapter Eighteen

But he did want to see her. He wanted an explanation. No. He wanted to understand, his eyes on the newspapers, all of them, as he read page after page of gossip, innuendo but little or no fact.

She'd stayed at Louis de Gerai's house in Paris. His wife had looked after her like her own daughter until she'd betrayed her friendship; until she'd walked in and found them in bed. Was that the truth? He'd thought her different. He wouldn't have thought her capable of such deceit. But what did he know? He'd seen her with his own eyes but what had he actually seen, as he brushed the waiter away with a wave of his hand. He'd seen the Frenchman from the back and the flicker of her dress, that's all. He hadn't seen her. He'd heard the soft mellifluous tone of his voice just as he'd heard his honeyed words, words he'd never have the nerve to speak.

He picked up his cup and took a sip of the cooling coffee with a grimace before opening The Sun. He'd already devoured the broadsheets, all of them before throwing them aside much to the chagrin of the head waiter. He might as well know the worst as he read the headlines.

It all goes tits up for Lady Titania.

Not the most original of captions but eye catching all the same as he examined the photo. In truth there was little to see. A hand on a leg – he was right about her having great legs. An arm around her waist but her face was averted. He wanted to see her face, to see her expression; to read her eyes. He'd see the truth in her eyes but in each shot she'd turned away just in time.

His eyes flickered over the words but there was nothing new. His wife had known all about their little affair and, now she had evidence, she was all set to take him to the cleaners. The press conveniently turning up was all a little contrived, as he took an absentminded bite of his toast. The wife must have set detectives on him. Either that or someone had tipped the media off, someone like Julietta.

'Have you finished, Lord Brayely? Perhaps I could bring you more toast, or another newspaper?' the waiter said, his expressionless face wandering over the crumpled pile.

'No, that's fine. Thank you,' he added, his smile brief. 'If you could arrange for my bill to be sent up? I'm leaving at once.'

He'd pick her up from Hamilton's and bundle her back to Scotland and marry her, his mind in overdrive. Pulling out his phone he put a call through to Toddy while he took the stairs two at a time. He'd pack, pay the bill and then kidnap her if she didn't want to go with him.

But he couldn't kidnap someone who wasn't there. He couldn't hijack her up to Scotland when he couldn't even find her. She'd disappeared. She'd disappeared into thin air despite every newspaper man (and woman) across the kingdom having her within their sights. The family on the ground floor told him in halting English she'd snuck out the back gate about ten minutes before he'd arrived. Hamilton hadn't been forthcoming and, when he'd finally phoned her parents, the conversation with her father had been difficult. They knew nothing or, at least, that's what they were admitting. His father was distraught but, apart from advising him to hire a good lawyer for breach of promise there was little he could say. Where could she hide? Where could she go with her face splashed across every newspaper in the country? She was hiding, that's for sure but nobody seemed to know where. The obvious answer was she'd left the country but her passport was sitting in the top drawer of her dressing table where she'd left it.

Flinging his case into the back of his car, he revved the engine and headed for home because he had nowhere else to go. They'd had something special and yet they'd both blown it, although he'd blown it first. He should've told her right from the beginning he'd fallen in love with her but he couldn't. At first he hadn't realised and when he had, he'd been too scared history would repeat itself. He crunched the gears. History had repeated itself. He'd been cuckolded for the second time; not a pretty thought but the truth all the same. His first wife had cheated on him and now Tansy had cheated on him. If only she'd been honest. If only she'd told him the truth about Paris.

He still didn't know for sure but the smug expression on the middle-aged chef's face said a lot, more than any words. If Tansy had slept with him, it wouldn't have been Tansy's fault. He would have manipulated her into bed and it wouldn't have been the first time as a trail of other women, other former employees and protégés, started coming out of the woodwork to add to his wife's testimony of his infidelities. He was the proverbial lech and Tor felt sick to his stomach that this man had ever laid his big greasy hands on his beautiful girl. He felt sick he'd doubted her even for one second as he raced up the M6 heading north. But he only had himself to blame. He shouldn't have let her go. He should've stayed with her. He should have made her explain.

He arrived at Castle Brayely just after midnight having telephoned ahead to Toddy to leave the outdoor lights on. Her ladyship was away on another one of her jaunts so he didn't expect anybody to be waiting for him. Just like last time, he walked into the kitchen with only the ghost of a memory to greet him; the ghost of a girl with snow-white skin and hair as black as night. There was no leftover toad in the hole waiting for him in the fridge and no freshly baked bread in the larder, only a choice of sliced white or sliced brown, which caused him to wrinkle his nose up before selecting a couple of thin slices. Slapping his cheese sandwich down on the bare wood alongside a bottle of whisky, he plonked himself into a chair and placed his head in his hands. He didn't know what to do anymore. He had no idea where to find her or even if she'd speak to him. Without her, he was less than nothing.

Finally, ignoring both the sandwich and the whisky he made his way up to his cold empty room; cold and empty despite Toddy having set up a heater in the corner. He didn't bother to get undressed. Instead, he dropped his leather jacket where it fell on top of his boots before flopping himself across the bed, face down and wished himself to sleep.

No one could have been more surprised at the bright shards of light sneaking through the curtains or the fact his watch told him it was 10 am. He didn't know what time he'd finally drifted off but it must have been when daybreak was peering over the horizon. Heading for the shower he stripped off the rest of his clothes and allowed the hot water to revive him before putting on his oldest jeans and t-shirt. After breakfast he'd have to think again. He could always ask Nanny or even Mary if she had any idea where she'd gone, but first he needed to eat as he leapt down the stairs with more energy than he'd had in a long time. If he'd been braver, he'd have attempted to slide down the highly polished bannisters, something he used to do with boring regularity until adulthood demanded a different set of behaviour. He'd almost decided to give it a go and had even hitched up his jeans in preparation when he eyed Todd watching him from the bottom.

'Any chance of breakfast? I know it's a bit late…'

'It'll be a few minutes; I'll just go and wash my hands,' he said, placing his fingers around the newel post. 'You should have, you know. I'd have picked you up if you'd fallen off.'

'Always there to get me out of difficulties,' Tor replied, clapping him on the back. 'Did you manage to find out about…?'

'Aye, I've left the information beside your side plate.'

'Great, thank you. I'll follow, if I may? There's something I want to ask you, and Mary if she's about or has she gone with my mother?'

'She's away with your mother. I've just been to collect the eggs so scrambled on toast alright?'

'I'm not sure I can stomach the plastic bread.' He pulled a grimace as he placed his hand on the older man's shoulder. 'She spoilt us for bread.'

She spoilt me for more than bread. She spoilt me for any other woman, he added silently.

'That she did,' he said, holding the baize door open to let Tor go first.

Chapter Nineteen

'How can you not believe me?' She watched her father shoot her mother a look from behind the security of The Evening Standard. 'What? What aren't you telling me?'

'Nothing, darling, it's you who've been keeping secrets, not us.'

'I don't believe you. Louis, or that bitch of a wife of his has been here, I just know it. You've struck some kind of deal, or something,' as she flitted between their embarrassed glances. 'There's something, I just can't put my finger on…' She flopped back in her chair, her gaze now on the guilty blush snaking across her mother's cheek and she felt sick to her stomach at the sudden realisation as to what they'd done.

'You knew, you knew all along this was going to happen,' her look incredulous. 'Those photographs were only incidental. You were happy to sell me off to the highest bidder. He'd have known nothing about me being cited as co-respondent until the headlines struck. How could you do this to your own daughter, how could you? It's like something out of Jane Eyre.'

'Hodd, if you could leave the room and close the door?' her mother said with an imperious hand wave. She only continued speaking when the door had settled back on its well-oiled hinges.

'Marielle came to see us and warned us what she was going to do as a curtesy to our friendship so, yes, we did know you were going to be cited and, yes, that did prompt, or should I say, hasten the meeting Tor's dear mother and I had planned. He has been married before, you know, so, in a way he's second-hand goods too.'

'Second-hand goods. How dare you.' She pushed herself back from the table and studied her parents. Her father, his neat balding head still hidden behind the paper, but she knew he was on tenterhooks the way his hands hadn't turned a page in well over five minutes. Her mother, in her powder blue twin-set and pearls, pearls that had been handed down through generations of Nettlebridges'. Surely she must have been adopted? Surely to goodness she couldn't be related to this pair? No, she shook her head. It was indisputable; she'd seen the baby photos. She was part of this pair with their supercilious ways and inconsiderate behaviour. She was tied to them by her birth certificate, bank account and title but at least now she knew the truth. At least now she knew it was as she'd thought all along; they were a conniving pair of manipulative old fogies who placed their own interests above that of their daughter's.

She hadn't been to blame. She'd been naive. She'd been stupid not to lock her bedroom door but she hadn't been to blame. There was nothing she'd either said or done that he could have misconstrued as an invitation into her bed. If it hadn't been for the fact she'd gone to sleep flicking through Mrs Beeton's Book of Household Management, all two thousand pages of it and in hard copy, an eighteenth birthday present from Hamilton, goodness knows what would have happened. As it was, Marielle walked in to find him rolling about the floor clutching his groin. She'd ended up taking him to hospital for emergency surgery thus providing her a window of opportunity too good to miss. She'd stuffed what she could into her rucksack and hailed a taxi, her cookery book clutched to her chest. It had never been far from her side since.

Her hands grasped the back of the chair as she remembered something she'd forgotten when Hamilton had told her about her supposed role in the divorce. If she could subpoena Louis's health records there was

bound to be a record of his operation.
There'd be some jumped up excuse as to the cause but at least it was something. She even had the book, a little battered it was true, but she'd happily give it over for forensic testing or whatever it was called, her brows pulled into a frown.

'Is Isaac still working for your solicitors?'

'What was that?'

'Isaac?' She sighed, trying to contain her annoyance. 'Is he still working for **Messrs. Pike, Pidgeon & Prue?**'

'Yes dear, although I have no idea what that's to do with anything?' her mother said, reaching for her spectacles. 'By the way, Nanny will be leaving us at the end of the week.'

'Nanny will be what?'

'I do wish you'd listen, darling. We've kept her well past her sell by date but it's now time for her to retire. She is sixty-six after all.'

'That's nothing these days.'

'It is if you're as arthritic as she is. Your father had to help her up the stairs yesterday as it was Hodd's day off; most inappropriate in addition to being most inconvenient. We were entertaining members of The Cabinet when Clemmy came and fetched him. The PM didn't know where to look, and as for The Chancellor of the Exchequer…'

But Tansy had had enough. With a brief excuse, she raced upstairs to find out just what had been going on during the few short weeks of her absence.

Nanny was ensconced in her usual chair with a book on her lap when Tansy burst through the door.

'Well, well, there's a sight for sore eyes and no mistake,' she said, placing the book on the table and picking up her knitting. 'I take it you've heard my news,' she added, shooting her a look under beetling brows.

'And I take it you've heard mine?' she tossed back, careful to ask Haggis's permission to sit next to him by proffering a cautious hand, a hand he studiously ignored as he carried on performing his morning ablutions.

'A stuff of nonsense. I didn't believe one word and neither should your parents...'

'The least said about them, the better. In fact, I've been wondering if I'm too old to divorce them or is that something they just do in America? I'll have to remember to ask Mr Pidgeon when I see him.'

'Aye, you do that, although I think he'll laugh himself daft,' she said, starting on a new row.

Tansy watched her in silence for a moment, this softly spoken woman she'd known all her life. It was probably selfish but she'd always hoped she'd be around forever, and she'd not just hoped. She'd just assumed when she finally got around to starting a family, Nanny would be on hand to advise her on the finer points of childcare. But now… but now, with no man on the horizon apart from Tor, a man who wouldn't marry her if she was the last woman in Scotland, there'd be no babies. She certainly wouldn't consider having them with anyone else so it was time for a life rethink. She'd start again. She'd managed to make a go of it at The Shard so there was no reason she couldn't somewhere else; somewhere far away, as far away from the reach and influence of her parents as possible. Scotland was probably far enough, but the other side. She had her credit card back and money in the bank, not forgetting Violet, her cerise pink Mini. The one thing she didn't have was any company…

'So, enough about me, what are you going to do?'

'Me, oh I'll be fine. I have a little put aside and my pension. Don't you worry about me,' her voice quiet.

'But I do, I can't help it. After all you've done for them, for us.'

'They don't see it like that. I'm just an inconvenience. If my hip hadn't stuck, I'd have managed the stairs fine but it did so there's an end to it.' She reached up a hand and patted her hair before picking up her needles again, only to set them back on her lap with a sigh, her eyes now fixed on Haggis.

'The only thing I'm worried about is Haggis; he is nearly eighteen after all. Your parents wouldn't want him and I'm not sure I'll be able to take him. He's such a proud beast, too proud to settle just anywhere.'

Tansy followed the direction of her gaze where he'd finished his wash and was now lying on his back, all paws in the air. 'I see what you mean. I'm tempted to tickle him but I have too much respect for my fingers, being as I'd probably never see them again.'

'He's not that bad.'

'Bad, of course he's bad. He's completely wicked but I do have a soft spot for him so he can come too.'

'Come too? Come where?'

Oh, I thought I'd told you. I'm going on a road trip and you and Haggis are coming.'

They set off almost immediately. With the help of Mr Hodd and Clemmy and much to the displeasure of her parents, they'd packed their bags before helping Haggis into his state-of-the-art cat basket.

'But you can't leave just like that, Nanny. I wanted you to repair my pink Elsa Schiaparelli for next weekend's party at The Ivy. You can go straight after.'

'If it will help any, I'll lend you a needle and thread, mam,' she said, her head held high as she made her way out the front door.

'Well, really.'

'No, you deserved that and more, mother. That woman has been dedicated, loyal and willing and you've just discarded her like an old rag.' Tansy said, slinging her rucksack across her back before picking up the cat basket. 'Come on Haggis, we know when we're not wanted.'

*

'I think you should go back.'

'I'm sorry?'

'Tansy, I think you should go back to Oban or, at least tell the viscount what you've just told me and Mr Pidgeon.'

'I don't think I can…'

'Well I do,' Nanny remarked, strapping herself in before turning in her seat to check on Haggis.

They'd pulled into a service station after their visit to see the solicitor. They had a long drive ahead but trying to persuade an intractable cat he really should spend a penny and stretch his legs was a feat of both patience and ingenuity. Finally a trip to the café for a tuna sandwich was called for.

'Such a waste of good tuna,' Nanny tutted, but with a smile on her face as she watched Tansy enticing him outside. 'It's a good job he's used to wearing a lead and no mistake.'

It was after they'd settled back in the car with a bag of sandwiches and crisps for the journey that Nanny started having a go.

'He has a right to know what happened in Paris. If what Mr Pidgeon says is true they'll want to keep that chef's trip to hospital and the subsequent injuries to his privates' private, excusing the pun. So he'll never get to hear the truth. Your name will be dropped as co-respondent and he'll always be left wondering what if.' She reached across and patted her leg. 'There's nothing worse than regretting the 'what if's' of life, love.'

Tansy tapped Oban into the Sat Nav with reluctant fingers. She'd do as she was told and then they'd scoot across to the other side of Scotland and find somewhere to call home.

'What was your greatest regret, Nanny?' she questioned softly, as she started the engine and headed onto the M6.

'Me? Well, now. That was a long time ago. There was a man, a good man but I decided I needed to see the big wide world. In them days, there were no fancy jobs going out abroad. In them days I wanted London, nothing else would do. I wanted to stand outside Buckingham Palace and steal a glimpse at the guards in them fancy hats. I wanted to walk around Piccadilly and feed the birds. I wanted to do all those things. I did all those things, but I did them alone. Toddy was the only man for me but I didn't know it at the time.'

'Toddy?'

'Aye, Toddy. It's a long time since that name has passed my lips,' she reminisced. 'He had the most amazing brown hair tied back in a ponytail and the clearest blue eyes.'

'Really?' Tansy hid a grin as she wondered if the balding Mr Todd could ever have had a ponytail. It was true he had lovely clear blue eyes but the chances of them being one and the same were so astronomical she decided not to dwell on it.

'He sounds a real looker.'

'He was. I've often wondered if he ever settled down. But it hasn't been all doom and gloom, lass. I've always had to work hard but hard work never hurt anyone. You're cooking, now there's a thing. Do you think you'll get that cookery book back from Mr Pidgeon after he's used it for evidence? A fine heavy book that,' she said, starting to giggle until the tears streamed down her face.

They arrived in Oban with no plans. Haggis was yowling as if in pain and, well, he might be after eight hours, give or take the odd stop every two hours or so. It was cold, dark and almost ten o'clock when Tansy almost automatically pulled on to the drive of the castle simply because she was out of ideas as to what to do with him. No self-respecting hotel would take them in so it was ask for help at the castle or spend the night in the car.

Chapter Twenty

'Good morning, Lord Brayely. What would you like for breakfast?' Tansy said, continuing to knead the dough in front of her.

He stood in the entrance to the kitchen and stared. The earth telescoped and light dimmed. Space, time, the present and past muted and merged. There was Tansy and Tor, nothing and no one else mattered in this, their little world of two.

Toddy, after one look, disappeared backwards through the baize door with a beam on his face. They didn't notice.

'For breakfast, sir? she repeated.

'Whatever's going.'

'Porridge with some bacon for afters?'

'That'll be fine; I'll have it here, if I may, at the end of the table?'

'It's your house.'

Actually it's a castle. Actually it's our castle. Actually it's our home.

But all he did was pull a chair back and sit down, his eyes watching as she collected eggs from the basket and started cracking them against the side of the pan. He'd been so scared, so afraid he'd never find her; that he'd never find the happiness and peace he'd found only with her. She was good at hiding, at running away so she must have wanted to be found. He knew in his heart it had to be lies, all lies but the doubts remained until just now; until…

'What the hell is that!' Glancing down he found himself being pummelled by a large tabby with very sharp claws before he finally turned his back and settled down to sleep.

Abandoning the eggs she went to his side.

'Now why won't he ever do that for me?' she grumbled, reaching out a gentle hand and getting a low throated growl for her efforts.

'I didn't know we had a cat?' he said, shooting out a hand and imprisoning her, his arm sneaking around her waist.

'We don't. It belongs to Nanny Mac.'

He blinked. 'And just why would you bring Nanny's cat all the way up here, won't she miss him?'

'No, silly. She's here too. It's a very long story.'

'Is it indeed? What's he called then?'

'Haggis, but I'd be careful. He's a spiteful beast.'

'No you're not, are you boy?' he said, tickling him under the chin. 'Now, I have some business with Tansy so hop off like a good chap and go find me a mouse,' he added, helping him to the floor with a stroke.

'I don't believe it,' her eyes wide.

'Neither can I,' he said, pulling her on to his lap and wrapping both arms around her before snuggling his face into her neck, his lips starting a little exploration all of their own.

'I thought I'd lost you after…'

'Never that, my love,' she whispered. 'I have to tell you what happened before...'

But he interrupted. 'You don't have to tell me a thing.'

'I do,' her body stiffening. But he wouldn't let her move away, his arms tightening even as his hands started massaging her back.

'Tell me then, but make it quick.'

'It's all lies, all of it,' her breathing laboured as his hand roamed up under her t-shirt.

'I know it is, my darling,' his lips now against the silky skin of her neck.

'Shush. Let me continue. I can't think when you do that.'

'Would you like me to stop?' His lips were now hovering over the little pulse hammering at the base of her throat.

She managed a shake of her head, her cheeks warming. 'She did find us in bed together...'

'Tansy, it's in the past. I don't mind,' even though he did; he minded dreadfully.

'Well, I do, so shut up until I've finished or else I'm leaving.' He felt a shudder run along her skin and hugged her to his chest; his lips, his hands, his breath now still.

'I was asleep. I was asleep and he got into bed with me. He said he loved me... I hit him with my Mrs Beeton so hard I...'

'You hit him...?'

'He had to have emergency surgery.'

He swallowed a laugh as he remembered the poker. His darling brave girl.

'I love you so much, but I do have a question, just one. Who the hell is Mrs Beeton?'

Epilogue

'Who would have believed it?'

'I know, my darling. But the way to look at it is you're not so much losing a butler as gaining a cook. Who do you think I learnt my love of cooking from?'

'Your mother?' His eyes crinkled up with laughter at the sight of Lady Nettlebridge holding on to the side of the rib for dear life. She'd already lost her designer hat to an erstwhile seagull and, now the wind had picked up she'd have to endure the bumpiest of journeys back to Seil.

'My mother! In your dreams, my lord. My mother wouldn't even know chickens laid eggs.'

'Ah, that's where you get it from, I often wondered.' He said, starting to tickle her around the waist.

'Get what from,' failing to bat his arm away as she dissolved into a fit of giggles.

'Your, er, prowess with animal husbandry.'

'You said you'd never mention that again.'

'Did I? I must have a very short memory, Lady Brayely,' he murmured, his hands moving from her waist to her shoulders. 'When was the last time I said I love you?'

She looked at her watch. 'About five minutes ago.'

'That long,' his lips meeting hers in the sweetest of kisses.

'How long do you think it will be before the rib gets back?' she said after a time, nestling under his arm as they stared out across the Sound of Kerrera, her shoes starting to slip on the shale at her feet.

He'd arranged the most beautiful surprise of a wedding on the island of Belnahua. He'd put Toddy on the case before he'd even proposed, for the third and final time, that morning in the kitchen.

Apart from her parents and his mother there were only the servants who, even now, were weaving their way back to the castle for a champagne reception. But Tor had asked her to wait until the last boat. It was just them, the building wind and the odd seagull for company. She didn't want for anything else.

'Tomorrow morning.'

'Tomorrow morning?' she said, her eyes widening. 'So you mean to tell me my parents and your mother are…'

'Expecting us to host a champagne reception back at the castle and we're not going to be there?' he replied, stamping a kiss against her lips. 'My mother and your parents don't need us, and we certainly don't need them.' He held her hand and started leading her up the beach.

'But if it hadn't been for them we would never have met?'

'We'd already met, my darling. Remember that sludge? I'll never forget it,' his hand now fingering the tulle of her dress. 'You were wearing white too with the cutest knee length socks,' his eyes now on her legs where the calf length skirt floated over her skin. 'Have I told you how beautiful you are?' he whispered, his gaze lingering on the tartan sash, his family tartan sash she'd cinched around her waist.

'Several times,' she laughed. 'But I'm happy for you to tell me again.'

'Minx.' He scooped her up in his arms and carried her right on up to the second of the cottages before nudging the door open with his foot and setting her down just over the threshold.

'We're staying here?' she questioned, her eyes roaming over the familiar and yet different room. There was a fire in the grate for a start and matting on the floor, and someone had cleared away all the cobwebs. There was even a table in the centre with a couple of camp chairs and candles everywhere she looked.

'There's no water or electricity, I'm afraid but there is champagne and food in the cool-box,' his hand now fiddling with his tie before tucking it in his pocket and removing his jacket.

There was also a bed, or at least a large mattress on the floor, its white sheets scattered with rose petals.

'Really? I'm starving,' she answered, turning away and making towards the table. But before she got one step she found herself twisted round, his hand on her chin as he stared into her face.

'Starving or shy, my love?' he said, rubbing his finger over her lower lip with a sensual familiarity.

'A little of both,' her eyes not quite meeting his.

He sighed and stepped back, his hand lingering on hers a moment before placing it back in his pocket.

'How about I go for a walk so you can, er...' he said, turning his back and walking to the door.

The one thing she didn't want was to be left alone but how could she tell him? How could she tell him she was scared more than anything and yet what was there to be scared of? This was Tor, moody as hell and with the sharpest of tongues but also the sweetest, kindest man she'd ever met. There'd been no harsh words since the day she'd returned. There'd been no arrogance and no moods, unless loving was a mood? Oh, she knew in the future there'd be moods and rows but there'd always be love first; his love for her and hers reaching up to join it.

She removed his tartan first and draped it across the bed with a gentle hand. Reaching up behind her back she pulled the zip on her Ayreshire lace and tulle vintage gown, letting it drop to the floor in a swathe of fabric. Next she slipped off one of her white satin shoes and, raising her leg catapulted it so hard across the room it banged against the door before landing at his feet.

She watched him bend down and cradle the flimsy trifle in his hands.

'I once said I wasn't Cinderella. I lied.'

He turned, his expression stunned as he took in her white corset with matching bra, panties, suspender belt and silk stockings.

'I'm not sure Cinderella would have worn those things under her dress,' he said, bending down to put her shoe on before stepping into the circle of her arms. 'Wasn't she poor or something?'

'Those things, as you call them are made from top of the range Belgium lace imported at great expense.' She laughed.

'Mmm and very nice to,' his hands now joining his eyes, his finger tracing the intricate pattern and the soft swell peeking out the top. 'We can ask Nanny to include some in the christening gown,' he added, reaching round the back to the fastening. 'Talking of which, I do hear practice makes perfect where babies are concerned and, as we only have a little over twelve hours…' his mouth lowering to hers.

The End

Acknowledgements.

There's lots of people to thank but firstly I'd like to thank you, the reader, for taking a chance on a relative unknown. I've had some lovely Amazon feedback from people around the world, people I'll never get to thank except here, so thank you Dawn McCaulay and Alice I Wynne to name just a couple.

I'd like to express my thanks to Adele Blair for agreeing to read a very early, second draft and for her encouraging comments, which gave me the faith to carry on. Also thanks to my street team for all your support and friendship.

I've had lots of help with this as I've never been to Oban. My husband spent a week there many years ago and thanks therefore must go to him, and for coming up with the fab name Hamilton. Talking about Hamilton, I'd also like to thank Oban resident, Lucy Hamilton (coincidence) for all the help. Lucy pointed me in the direction of Belnahua... For amazing photographs of Oban and the surrounding area why not check out her Instagram account (loosemooose). I'd also like to thank Gregor MacKinnon from The Manor

House (Oban) and Dawn from The Oyster Bar (Seil).

Mary Doyle, thank you for letting me borrow your name. I hope you like her?

Amy Potter, thank you for telling me about a *Balayage,* I'd never heard of it but now I want one too.

Finally love, as always, to my three wonderful children for putting up with me…

I love hearing from readers. You can find me on Twitter (not a lot) Instagram (occasionally) and Facebook (too much).

Now, book number three is a little different – a little darker… You'll find the start on the next pages and a large print version will be available soon.

Jenny O'B

NB: Professionally edited to UK English.

Knicker: - UK slang for pound notes

Song: All about the Bass, by the wonderful Meghan Trainor – we know all the words…

Printed in Great Britain
by Amazon